Paul the Pillow Monster

Brian Clopper

PublishAmerica
Baltimore

© 2004 by Brian Clopper.

All rights reserved. No part of this book may be reproduced, stored in a retrieval system or transmitted in any form or by any means without the prior written permission of the publishers, except by a reviewer who may quote brief passages in a review to be printed in a newspaper, magazine or journal.

First printing

ISBN: 1-4137-1333-5
PUBLISHED BY
PUBLISHAMERICA, LLLP.
www.publishamerica.com
Baltimore

Printed in the United States of America

THE SETTING:
The MAGICAL REALM of CASCADE*

When mortal belief in magic began to die out, the magical and mythological creatures of Earth found their life forces fading. Rather than face apathy and extinction, they banded together and migrated to another dimension where their combined powers could sustain them, a magical haven called Cascade. There they thrived, and a multimystical society was born.

*If you like the patchwork world of Cascade, be sure to check out Piers Anthony's Xanth novels. They were a thrill to read when I was a kid.

CHAPTER ONE
POMP AND CIRCUS AUNTS

"I HATE WEARIN' PURPLE! It's not at all a royal color," grumbled Max, the taller of the two monsters. Max and Paul stood in front of a large mirror inspecting their robes. The garments were solid purple with golden fringe on the sleeves. As they eyed each other wearing identical robes in the mirror, their physical differences became even more magnified.

Max had all the grace of a rhino. His bulk extended from his immense padded feet all the way up to his large, bony head topped with two rows of blunt horns. He would appear quite intimidating if it weren't for his tiny mouth graced with fangs that seemed almost an afterthought to his long face. His thick arms hung at his side, extending past his knees. One could imagine his knuckles dragging if he slouched any farther.

Of course, most tall beings, monsters included, are slouchers. Imagine if virtually everyone else in your life was shorter than you. Glancing at how small Paul was next to Max, you could easily account for Max's poor posture.

Paul, even covered in a graduation robe, couldn't hide his slender build. Bordering on scrawny, for which he had received his share of ridicule, Paul's body was quite the opposite of his friend's.

To further showcase their differences, Paul's orange scales, tiny fins and webbed hands and feet revealed his aquatic heritage, while it was quite obvious that Max's green smooth skin and husky build detailed his origins as strictly land-bound.

Max said, "We make a frightful couple, don't we?"

Paul produced a thin smile.

"Hard to believe the two of us are graduating with honors, huh?" Max hated silence and always attempted to fill conversational voids with statements of the obvious.

Paul was struggling to mount his graduation cap over the nest of spikes centered on his head while glancing nervously at the grandfather clock to his right. "We'd better hurry or we won't make it to the main hall in time."

Max smirked, "Ah, let 'em wait for us. They won't start without their class valedictorian, will they?" He slapped Paul soundly on the back.

Paul frowned. "Watch it. You almost squished Treek."

A tiny creature, looking like a cross between a lobster and a cobra, popped its head out of Paul's collar. Treek hissed at Max.

"You brought your pet to graduation? Better hope Headmaster Stevens doesn't catch you," said Max.

"He won't. Remember, I took Treek on that field trip to Behemoth Bay, and no one knew. Treek's good at staying undercover, aren't you, boy?" Paul scratched at the peach fuzz that rimmed his pet's chin. Treek cooed, then slipped back inside his owner's gown.

Max shrugged his large shoulders as he made final adjustments to his own cap. "Suit yourself, but I'm sure glad he's not rooting around in my robes. That's gotta be a little ticklish."

"A little, but I'll manage."

"Famous last words," muttered Max as he took a minute to sweep over his outfit with a lint brush. Satisfied he looked presentable, the monster twirled to face Paul and kneeled on one knee. He bowed and presented the brush to his monster friend as if it were a treasured sword about to be blessed.

****

The main hall of the Monster Academy had hosted every graduation ceremony for the 76 years the school had been in operation, except the first two. Graduation had been held in the Fear Fields to the north of the campus, a tradition that quickly ended when the second graduation was interrupted by the ill-timed appearance of a pack of kraken wolves. These large, hairy beasts looked like a twisted experiment any of Cascade's four registered mad scientists might concoct. Imagine a wolf the size of a tractor trailer with ten tentacles and see-through skulls. These natives of Cascade had developed an appetite for the fear berries the monsters harvested from the fields.

Take a pack of hungry, temperamental kraken wolves, place over a thousand folding chairs occupied by proud monster relatives between them and their supply of fear berries, and you can begin to imagine the horrible results.

The cathedral ceiling of the main hall was decorated with a murky painting depicting the world's first monsters rising out of the Great Darkness. Eight oak columns divided the room, allowing a wide walkway between their large bases. Creepy-crawly vines decorated each column. Will-o-wisp lanterns hovered in the air—powered by the bright magical spirits swirling about inside.

In contrast to the rich details of the ceiling and columns, the floor, or lack thereof, disappointed Paul. The main hall was the only building in the academy with dirt floors. He didn't know the reason, but assumed it had something to do with the nature of so many monsters who drew power from the earth. His Aunt Josephine was always remarking on the old power held in the ground. To Paul, dirt was dirt—something to be cleared away.

Paul craned his neck backward to look for his family.

Max, sitting to his left, elbowed him. "Give it up. Even I can't see my family over all those antlers, horns and antennae, and they stick out like sore thumbs normally. My mom's half giant. Have I ever mentioned that?"

Paul continued to look for his parents as the orchestra began playing. The tune, "A Monster's Waltz," filled the room with notes of sadness and an air of dignity. "These aren't the best seats."

Max nearly throttled him. Shaking Paul, Max said, "Are you kidding me? We've got front row seats. We can see everything we need to see. You only graduate once, Paul. Enjoy it."

Paul remarked, "I know, I know. I just don't want to look at the stage because I have to get up there soon and give my, you know, speech."

Max chuckled as he cocked his head to listen to his favorite part of "A Monster's Waltz." He offered reassurance to his friend. "What happens, happens. Soak it up and roll with the punches."

"Easy for you to say. You don't have anything to prove." Paul fiddled with the scroll in his hand. He had written his speech out on the aged paper his father had given him. On one side of the scroll were his words. On the other side was the speech his father had given at his own graduation over 20 years ago. His father had offered the scroll to him as a gift of pride. Two generations of valedictorians in one family was a rare honor. His father thought it only fitting that Paul write his speech on the same paper as his own. It would be a family heirloom. Paul felt otherwise about the yellowed document. Everything had to be perfect, like his dad wanted.

"Close your eyes and just listen," said Max.

Paul did as his friend requested. Sadly, having transparent

eyelids didn't help to block out the distractions. Still, he tried to zero in on the music, attempting to find his quite shy sense of calm. The final chorus of the song was lilting through the hall. Paul felt the music vibrating through the air thanks to his sensitive eyebrows. His eyes drifted up to a nearby will-o-wisp lantern. The two light spirits inside danced joyfully. Their glow pulsed to the rise and fall of the music. Just as Paul was finding himself engaged by the sights and sounds, the music trickled away. He looked up at the stage as silence descended throughout the room.

Headmaster Stevens, satisfied the music had been drained from the room, rose and strode across the stage. Striding is a relative term in the case of the headmaster. His short stature and rather large bottom, coupled with his grossly stick-like legs, resulted in a slight waddle. The headmaster tried to play it off as a source of pride, but he knew his students giggled and snickered at his platypus style of transport. He took his time as he walked to the podium. Carved to look like a dragon with outstretched wings, the podium dwarfed the tiny headmaster. Stevens nodded in approval at his assistant upon seeing the stool neatly propped up behind the podium and hidden from immediate sight. While he was not ashamed of his lack of height, he also felt it dignified to be seen by his audience. As he mounted the stool, his bushy whiskers brushed against the podium. The wooden furniture creaked as it turned to look at him.

The dragon podium glared at Stevens and whispered, "Hey, watch it with the mustache. That tickles."

"Hush," scolded the headmaster. Why his assistant had bought the talking podium was beyond him. She special ordered it from the Wizard Bailey. Since receiving something from the Wizard Bailey was an honor, Headmaster Stevens could not return the annoying podium without insulting Cascade's most powerful spellcaster.

"Maybe you should let me do the talking. I've been told I

have a way with words," offered the dragon, waving his wings coyly.

"If I wished the English language mangled, you'd be the first I'd seek," said Stevens. His cheeks were growing red with irritation.

The dragon pulled back and clutched his chest as if recoiling from an arrow wound. "Ouch, your tongue doth sting."

"Enough. Face forward and be silent," said the headmaster.

"Could I at least do your intro? Please?" the dragon fluttered his eyelids with much urgency.

"Will you shut up afterwards?" asked Stevens.

"Most definitely," said the podium.

"Very well. Just don't try to upstage me like you did last year. No breathing fire at the end, okay?" The headmaster buried his face in his palm.

"How about I conclude with a puff of smoke? At least give me that," said the dragon as it puffed out its wooden chest.

"Fine. Get it over with," said Stevens, rolling his eyes.

The dragon turned to face the audience. Over 2,000 filled the main hall, ranging from proud parents to distant relatives. Each was here to witness the graduation of a special someone.

The dragon cleared his throat. All eyes were on him. *Just the way I like it*, he thought. One of the perks to being a podium was getting to be the center of attention during major speaking events. The podium savored the moment. He closed his eyes and drew a deep breath. He exhaled and out poured the most thunderous introduction. "Friends and family from near and far, we are gathered to celebrate yet another class of dastardly monsters. These young beasties are about to enter the workforce as productive members of society. Each has been taught how to haunt, spook, bedevil and perplex the most jaded mortal. I've had the pleasure of meeting each of the students and I can safely say they are a frightening bunch."

A rumble of laughter rolled over the crowd.

The dragon continued, "It is my delight to introduce the

instructor responsible for turning these budding monsters into card-carrying creepies. I give to you today—" He paused, letting the anticipation simmer. "Headmaster Stevens!" As the words filled the air, so too did a billowy cloud of black smoke. It poured out of the dragon and blanketed the stage with its presence.

The main hall was thundering with applause, which was quite fortunate for Headmaster Stevens. It prevented the crowd of onlookers from hearing his terrible cough. The dragon's smoke had caused him to wheeze and gag, his eyes welling up with fat tears.

The dragon chuckled, "Maybe next time a little fire might not be a bad idea."

Stevens delivered a swift kick to the podium's tail as he waved his hands about, attempting to dissipate the lingering smoke.

Once relative silence returned to the main hall, Stevens had cleared enough of the air to allow him to begin his own speech. "Each of the past 56 years, I have stood proud among you with grace in my heart and...."

****

Paul tried to listen to the headmaster's speech, but he was having a hard time focusing. He knew it was important he show the headmaster the proper respect, as he was not exactly on good terms with the head of the academy. He had had several run-ins with Stevens during his five-year stay, and all had been the result of mischief and unfortunate accidents on Paul's part. Headmaster Stevens, while fully aware of Paul as an outstanding student, had little patience for the silly situations that seemed to stick to Paul like bubble gum.

Max leaned over to him. "Thinking of your last trip to his office, are ya?"

"Trying to forget it is more like it," said Paul.

"Ah, that was classic. I can't believe you took the blame for that fire elemental when it was clearly Snickety's fault." Max shot a glare back at the serpent in question. Snickety sat three rows back, glowering at his fellow classmates.

"I'd rather have Stevens mad at me than at Snickety," said Paul, shrinking down in his seat. He again tried to center his attention on the headmaster. The next part of the ceremony was the valedictorian's speech. The headmaster would introduce him, and Paul had to be ready.

"Yeah, you're definitely on shaky ground with Stevens. Wouldn't want to be you," said Max.

"Shhh," said Paul.

Ignoring his friend, Max remarked, "Hey, speaking of shaky ground, take a look." He pointed with his sausage-link fingers at the ground under his friend's webbed feet. "Looks like you have a visitor."

The dirt beneath Paul was churning and shuffling about. Something was unearthing itself and wasn't discreet about it. Every student in the front row had his eye or eyes directed at the ever softening ground near Paul. Even the headmaster paused to offer a glance. The dirt had caved in, presenting a hole no more than a foot or two in diameter.

"Please don't be an ancient evil. Please don't be an ancient evil," whispered Paul as he clasped his hands together to offer a prayer.

"Sure hope this main hall isn't built over a burial ground or something. I thought they surveyed for the walking dead before they built this place," said Max.

A plump head decked out with stringy, strawberry-red hair popped out of the hole. Three drill-shaped horns were evenly spaced atop the monster's head. The monster emerged from the hole and approached Paul. She was no taller than his knee, and Paul knew her instantly. "Aunt Josephine, you made it!" he said with glee. He jumped to the floor and gave her a big hug.

PAUL THE PILLOW MONSTER

Paul's aunt smiled, revealing deep dimples on her yellow skin. Aunt Josephine was a striking female—if you were looking for something to strike a large bell, that is. The squat body underneath her rich black dress bulged in the most unusual places. Her plump legs were thankfully covered by thigh-high boots featuring a polka dot pattern that would make any circus clown proud. Of course, each feature was secondary to her immense nose. Larger than her head, the proboscis in question was a definite conversation piece. As if to highlight the nose even more, a large red ball was mounted on its tip.

Max smiled and said, "Why, Paul, aren't you going to introduce me to such a radiant beauty?"

Paul looked over at Headmaster Stevens, who had resumed his speech. The headmaster's assistant, Ms. Lackee, was making a beeline for them. Paul was sure she had a suitably ripping scolding for him. The gorgon was even more unpleasant than the headmaster and was Paul's least favorite member of the staff.

"This is my Aunt Josephine," he said hurriedly to Max.

"Charmed, milady," said Max, cupping her outstretched hand in his own meaty palms.

"Who's the beefcake, nephew? What a dreamboat," she said, batting her long, straggly eyelashes his way.

"Um, that's Max. You really shouldn't have burrowed in here, Aunt Josie," said Paul. Ms. Lackee was only a couple yards away. The snakes in her hair shot Paul icy stares.

"Well, when I knew we were late, I just had to travel underground. It's so much faster—less traffic, you know. I meant to unearth outside of the main hall, but I must've miscalculated a little." She brushed clumps of soil out of her hair. "Of course, Jolene made us even later. Had to dig the tunnel wide enough to fit her blasted wings."

"Aunt Jolene is with you?" Paul asked.

"She should be whizzing out of the hole any second, hon." Aunt Josephine turned expectantly to look. "She brought our gift."

Ms. Lackee had arrived and was spewing her venomous scolding to all within earshot. "Paul Phineas Palligaster, you know guests must confine themselves to aisles 7-20 during the ceremony. Why, if Headmaster Stevens wasn't otherwise occupied, I'm sure he'd have a few sharp words for you."

Paul frowned. He knew what came next.

Ms. Lackee didn't disappoint. "I'm sure he'd tell you what an irresponsible, selfish little runt you are. He'd also probably comment on your utter lack of respect for tradition and on your annoying bright orange scales." Ms. Lackee, as a result of a freak accident involving Paul and Max, had lost her ability to turn others into stone. She had had it in for Paul ever since. He would've preferred her piercing stone gaze to her venomous tongue.

Her snake hair hissed at Paul as he returned to his seat. "Yes, ma'am."

"How dare you talk to my nephew in that manner, Gorgon!" said Aunt Josephine.

Ms. Lackee ducked down as Aunt Jolene flew out of the hole. Graced with long mosquito wings, Paul's other aunt was Josephine's polar opposite. Her salmon pink wings were only the tip of the iceberg in terms of her beauty. Her finely chiseled cheeks and chin were draped in pearly white skin that glittered with life. A constant halo of sparkles rimmed her golden hair. Her wide, blue eyes spoke of warm tea parties and chatty sleepovers. Where her sister had bulges and gathers, Jolene had none. Her contours were sweetly curved and covered with a modest skirt and turtleneck. A neat ivory tote bag clung to her side. The only indications she was a monster and had not stepped off the cover of a fashion magazine were her wings and the cluster of small horns that protectively crested her shoulders.

Max muttered, "Ugh, not much in the looks department, but we can't all be a gem like you, Aunt Josie. May I call you Josie?" He bowed to the shorter, squatter aunt.

Aunt Josephine giggled. "Oh, this one is a keeper, he is."

"Ladies, and I use that term loosely, if Headmaster Stevens was available, I'm sure he'd tell you to take your business elsewhere. He'd also comment on your utter lack of manners and undignified fashion sense." The gorgon eyed both aunts with distaste.

Aunt Jolene hovered over the gorgon. The snakes atop Ms. Lackee snapped at her. "Aren't we just a Catty Cathy? Sheath your claws, you second-rate Medusa, and mind your manners. My sister and I apologize for our entrance, but we will not put up with your insults."

Ms. Lackee clamped her mouth shut, as if she had just eaten a fish much too large for her mouth. Paul had never seen the headmaster's assistant at a loss for words.

"I'm sure if the headmaster was here, he'd accept our apology and ask us to finish our business with our nephew without making a further scene. Am I right?" said Jolene, mimicking Ms. Lackee's tone to perfection.

Ms. Lackee looked over at her boss to see he had stopped his speech and was looking at her with distaste. She scanned the main hall to see all eyes on her.

Jolene leaned in closer and whispered, "What's the matter, dear? Snake got your barbed tongue?"

Ms. Lackee and her snakes burst into tears as she bolted toward the back of the stage.

Aunts Jolene and Josephine patted each other on the back and laughed. "She's quite the snake in the grass, isn't she?" said Josephine.

"She's the one who made the asp of herself," cracked Jolene.

Paul looked over at his aunts. "Um, everybody's looking at you," he whispered.

"Of course they are. We've got the show in our blood. I'd kill for a spotlight right about now." Josephine looked about, expecting to see a spotlight present itself to her.

"What are they?" asked Max. "They seem to enjoy the awkward stares."

Paul replied, "They can't help it. They're my circus aunts. They haunt a circus and they love turning any place they visit into a three-ring event. The more astonished looks, the better."

"Paul, quite a place you got here. Almost as spacious as our beloved big-top," said Jolene.

Paul said, "You need to let them get back to the graduation. It's not time for a show, okay?"

Josephine, mocking Paul's whisper, said, "Okay, little one. We'll hold off on the flaming swords until later. It's your turn in the light, dear."

"Thank you," said Paul.

Josephine barked at her sister, who had been flitting about gathering all the will-o-wisp lanterns nearby. "Time to close the curtains, sis. No performance today."

Jolene's bottom lip puckered up. "But, Josie, I was making you a spotlight."

"No. Just give Paul his gift and tell everyone to get back to what they were doing," said Josephine.

The podium dragon, besides having the gift of gab, was also blessed with wonderful hearing and had registered the entire conversation. After all, it had been much more lively than listening to Stevens drone on and on. Sensing an opportunity to gather attention to himself and win back his boss's favor, the dragon's voice blazed with passion. "Thank you, ladies, for your fine performance." He turned to the audience and gestured upward with his hands. "Folks, give it up for our drama department. They were just displaying their talents for all of us to enjoy. Color me jealous, but I have to admire the natural talent that could eclipse even the oratory brilliance of our very own headmaster." The dragon looked to his boss for approval as the crowd cheered, chuckled and clapped.

Headmaster Stevens said, "Good, just no smoke."

The dragon whispered, "Okay."

PAUL THE PILLOW MONSTER

Headmaster Stevens waited for the chatter to die down again before continuing. "As you can see, our students bring many talents to the table. None more so than our class valedictorian. His cleverness, thirst for knowledge and excellent scores on the S.A.T. (Scare Aptitude Test) are only a fraction of the abilities hidden in this young monster. I present to you, Paul Phineas Palligaster, Suma Cum Laude!"

CHAPTER TWO
BURNING DOWN THE HOUSE

PAUL INCHED HIS WAY toward the stage. Max beamed at him, proudly pointing at him with both hands. "It's all you, baby," he said. "Deliver the goods."

Jolene shot into the air upon hearing Max. "Deliver! We came here to deliver!" She glanced around for her sister. Josephine was walking toward the back of the main hall. Jolene, herself, had drifted up above the lanterns, but had stayed within earshot of Paul and his friend.

She looked to her sister. Josephine's back was to her. Jolene knew better than to shout for her sister. She didn't want to cause another scene. Actually, she did. Being a show stealer was in her purple blood. "Now is not the time, Joey," she muttered to herself.

Jolene pulled a flower-and-fruit-laced wreath from her tote bag. She flew over to the stage, staying above the lanterns, out of the limelight. While the audience had not seen her, her flight plan did not escape her nephew's attention.

Paul looked up at his aunt. Equal parts frustration and fright dwelled on his face. "What are you doing?" he whispered harshly.

"Our gift, Paul. I have to deliver our gift to you." She held the wreath, taking measure of its weight.

"Can't it wait till after?"

"No, it's a tradition. You must wear the wreath when you give your marvelous speech." She added extra pout to her already pouty lips.

"Ugh, this family is way too mixed up with traditions," said Paul, crinkling his scroll.

"Please," she said, softening her thin eyebrows to deliver her most persuasive puppy dog look.

Paul held up his hands, flustered at losing control yet again. "Oh, all right, give it to me."

Jolene tossed the wreath at her nephew's head. It plummeted, landing neatly on his shoulders. Eying the wreath he now wore, he could tell his aunts had spent much time crafting it for him. He looked up at her and mouthed a kind and sincere thank-you.

Jolene blushed and replied, "You're welcome." She began to fly back to her vantage point, but offered one additional remark. "Paul, dear, feel free to eat it after the ceremony. Not only does it smell good, it's edible, too."

Paul walked to the podium. Meeting him halfway, Headmaster Stevens shook his hand. He whispered to the young monster, "Don't mess this ceremony up further, Palligaster, or else." He gave the valedictorian a deceivingly warm hug and walked to a set of chairs off to the side of the stage filled with fellow staff members.

Paul stepped up to the podium and climbed on top of the stool. The dragon podium made a comment. "Someone, please get a tall person up here to speak. Sheesh, are all monsters such little Napoleons?"

"Who?" said Paul.

"Never mind." The dragon clammed up.

Paul unrolled his scroll and began his speech. "My time here at the Monster Academy has been well spent. In addition to the knowledge and skill I have learned in the classroom and the friendships I have made...."

Paul bent forward. Treek, who had remained quite still throughout the ceremony so far, was stirring. His pet was huffing and twittering with urgency. He was also trying to make his way out of Paul's robe through his collar. "Treek, not now. Please, stay hidden," he whispered to his pet in his most soothing voice. Treek had wiggled his way up through the robe and was attempting to claw his way out. Paul pulled his scroll toward his chest to shield the audience from spying his pet's emerging head. With his free hand, he attempted to push the stubborn creature back into his robe.

"Please be a good little wormle and stay," he said.

Remembering he had a captive audience, Paul peeked over the scroll and announced, "Sorry, lost my place. Had to write small enough to fit all of the wonderful things I wanted to say about the academy on my scroll." He flashed a sheepish grin.

Treek had pulled his upper body up out of the robe and was working to remove his long serpent half as well. His eyes were focused on the wreath adorning his owner's neck. Something on the wreath had drawn the wormle's attention. Paul looked down to see, that among the flowers and other fruits, his aunts had garnished the gift with vines loaded down with brumbleberries, a wormle's favorite food.

"Oh no."

Unable to hold onto Treek, Paul gave up trying to hide his problem. His speech dropped to the stage as the monster jumped off the stool. Paul was attempting to remove the wreath as his pet feasted on the brumbleberries within reach. Afraid the wormle might claw him in its mad grab for food, Paul tossed the wreath. With a hungry wormle attached, it sailed through the air and landed at the feet of the podium.

The dragon's eyes grew wide. "Are those thrum-thrum cones on that wreath?" he blubbered.

Paul examined the wreath from a safe distance. "Um, I think they are. Why?"

The wooden dragon contorted his face as if his snout itched. His voice sounded a little stopped up. "I'm alwergic to thwum-thwums."

"Oh," said Paul.

"Thwey make me…" the dragon brought his hands up to cover his mouth. It was too late. Blasting forth from his mouth and nasal passages was the brightest plume of flames, even brighter than the will-o-wisp lanterns.

"Ah-CHOOOOOOOO!"

Panic descended on the main hall as the dragon continued to sneeze, lighting fire to the stage and several wooden columns.

Max rushed onto the stage and scooped up his buddy and pet. "C'mon, Paul. Time to evacuate." He flipped the monster over his shoulder and barreled out of the main hall.

"This isn't good," said Paul.

"You sure take after your aunts. That was one heck of a light show!" squawked Max. "You're a show stopper!"

Paul frowned. For the second time in the academy's history, a graduation had been flummoxed. Paul would much rather face a pack of kraken wolves than one lone, very irate headmaster.

CHAPTER THREE
CAREER PLACEMENT

THE WAITING ROOM TO the headmaster's office was sparsely decorated. The dark wood paneling overwhelmed everything. A single glass case hung from a chain in the middle of the room. Inside the display, a tattered first edition of *The Monster's Handbook* rested against a velvet book holder. Paul saw the cover of the leather bound volume was signed, but could not decipher the signature.

No chairs occupied the waiting room. Max and Paul stood as far away as possible from the only desk there. Ms. Lackee sat behind the simple black desk dictating a memo into a crystal ball. She spoke just loud enough for Paul and Max to hear.

"File #107. Perpetrators: Paul Phineas Palligaster and Maxwell Murble. Incident Title: Burning Down the Main Hall. Store in the mainframe crystal. Employee access limited to Headmaster Seymour Stevens and Ms. Lorelli Lackee. Patch a copy of file to Stevens's crystal ball." She stopped talking and turned to the two waiting monsters.

"Oh, please do go in. Don't want to keep him waiting. He gets quite unruly when people do that, especially repeat offenders." She hissed the last three words.

Paul and Max pushed open the heavy doors leading to the headmaster's office. Max grinned. "Hey, look, they polished the doorknobs since our last visit. I can see my reflection. Heh-heeh."

"Oh and, boys, please tell him to access his crystal ball so it'll record your meeting. When he gets all fire and brimstony, he tends to forget about the small things." Ms Lackee giggled in delight.

Max patted his friend on the back. "Hey, relax. What's the worst he can do? We've already graduated from the academy? It was an accident. Old Sourpuss has to understand that, right?"

"Why are you here, anyway?" asked Paul. "None of this was your fault."

"True, but a friend doesn't leave another friend to hang out and dry. Besides, if he has two people to blame, he's more likely to go easier on you, right?"

They walked down the long hall leading to the headmaster's office, ignoring the over twenty portraits of Stevens arranged in neat rows on either side of them. Each year after graduation, a new portrait was added. As they arrived at the door to the headmaster's office, both spared a glance at the last frame on the wall. It was marked with the current graduation year, but held no portrait.

Max said, "Looks like Seymour is a little behind schedule, huh?"

Without assistance, the double doors before them opened to reveal a very tiny office. It was no wider than it was deep, and no bigger than an ordinary bathroom. A large desk was crammed into the tiny space, and Paul imagined only about three people could fill the room at any one time.

Max said, "Gotta say, I don't understand why you don't knock down a wall here or there and make your office more livable, Headmaster. Given any thought to my suggestion to eat into the hallway a little and spread yourself out a bit?"

"Tradition," Stevens replied.

"Um, Ms. Lackee wanted me to remind you to access your orb, sir," said Paul, darting into the close quarters of the office as the doors squeezed shut behind them.

"Yes, we must follow procedures," said the headmaster, passing his hand over the large crystal ball before him. "Open File…" He paused, pondering the number.

"107," offered Max.

Paul gave him a look of surprise.

Max shrugged and said, "What? I listen." He turned his back to his friend and mumbled, "Sometimes."

Headmaster Stevens sat at his desk, repeating the number into the crystal ball. Other than the desk and the crystal ball, the only furnishing was a bookshelf that ran up the entire wall behind the desk. Shelf after shelf sat empty, deprived of books, denied even a single cobweb or piece of lint as an occupant.

"Not much of a reader, huh?" said Max.

"One has little need for books other than *The Monster's Handbook*." He tapped his temple with his bony forefinger. "And that? That I have committed to memory."

"Why not remove the bookshelves? That oughtta make a little room at least," said Max.

"Because, little monster…" Headmaster Stevens rose up out of his seat. Standing on his padded chair, he was still a few feet short of Max's height. The intensity of his stare displayed how little the difference in height mattered to him. "It's tradition. My father, the great Ignatius Fluttertop Stevens, had them built when he was headmaster."

Max stepped back from the headmaster as much as he could in the tight office. "Oh."

"Tradition is born from routine, from treasuring rules. When patterns are established, they must be regarded." The headmaster shared his grim stare with Paul as well.

Max snickered weakly. "Hey, that means what we're doing here is tradition then, right?"

Stevens arched his eyebrows, a gesture that demanded Max continue his thought.

"This is our what, fifth, sixth visit here? You chew us out, dole out a punishment, and we live with it. It's a pattern, huh?" said Max.

"Yes, sadly it is a pattern, but some patterns should be broken before they become traditions." Headmaster Stevens slid back into his chair.

"Sir, it was an accident, pure and simple. Max had nothing to do with it. I'm fully to blame," said Paul.

The headmaster scratched his chin and looked up at the ceiling, which seemed as distant as the sun or the moon. He gazed upward for a long time, a very long time.

Paul and Max trailed their eyes toward the ceiling. They soon realized they couldn't see the ceiling. No light greeted them from above, and the shadows swallowed up the meager walls of the office as they headed toward the sky.

Max said, "That's weird. I never noticed that before. Creepy." He looked around the office. "Hey, there's no window. How on earth is there any light in this place?"

Paul was equally baffled. No will-o-wisp lanterns, torches or glo-globes around. "I don't understand…"

"There is light in this office because tradition demands it be so. Tradition is powerful magic, don't you agree?" hissed the headmaster.

Both nodded solemnly.

Max added, "That's some powerful mojo."

Headmaster Stevens grimaced. "Yes, tradition is wonderful. At my academy, we have a tradition of sending our graduates out into the world, armed with skills and talents to assure them very rewarding jobs in the fright field. We pull no strings nor do we call in favors in locating jobs. We trust that to our graduates. They find the job that best suits them. We have 100% placement."

Max replied, "That's a great record. Good to know."

"We don't interfere in their careers. That's our tradition."

Paul and Max nodded.

"For the two of you, however, I'm starting a new, special tradition." The headmaster steepled his hands. "It's quite fitting, really. For all you've given to our school during your stay, it's the least we could do."

"Really, you don't have to go to any trouble," said Max.

"Oh, but I must. Your escapades, especially the glorious way you managed to burn down our most prized landmark, force me to treat you differently." The headmaster rubbed his forehead with exasperation. "You always manage to stand out."

Sensing bad news, Max chattered on nervously. "Honest, we don't need your help with jobs. My dad's got a great castle gig lined up for me, and Paul here, he's got several offers. Didn't you say your aunts had an opening at their circus for someone to spook the cannonballer? And didn't that old witch contact you last week about haunting a whole subdivision of goblin cottages?" He turned to Paul, urging him to fill the silence with any words he could muster.

"Uh…"

"Stop it!" shouted the headmaster. His brow was patterned with wrinkle upon wrinkle, announcing his displeasure to all within a mile radius.

Paul and Max huddled closer to each other. Paul said, "What are you doing to us?"

The headmaster ducked behind his desk, shuffled a few files in a drawer neither Max nor Paul could see, then resurfaced holding two folders.

"I've taken the liberty of finding jobs for you. I'd love to see you try and stand out now!" he said with a chill to his voice.

Max snatched both folders from him. "What have you done?"

Stevens sat back, gloating. "Your parents have signed off on this. They agree it would be a wonderful character builder. The contracts are all quite official and bind you to your jobs for a minimum of three years."

Paul grabbed his folder from his friend and scanned through its contents.

He looked in horror at the headmaster, then at Max. "I'm a pillow monster?! Nooooo!"

Max's bottom lip danced about, quivering to a rhythm of shame. "I've got you beat. I'm gonna haunt a sock drawer!"

Both monsters began to sob.

Headmaster Stevens leaned back into his chair and stared up at the empty bookcase and the location of his questionable ceiling.

Tradition is such a wonderful tool, he thought.

CHAPTER FOUR
NAME YOUR POISON

IT TOOK MUCH COAXING, but Paul finally convinced his parents to let him visit his friend, Bickyl, on the eve of his new job as a pillow monster. Truthfully, it was his mother who had reluctantly given him permission. His father had not talked to him since he had botched the graduation. Paul had spent the last week and a half wrestling with a bout of depression. He didn't want to be a pillow monster, one of the lowest forms of fright work, but he was also filled with enough guilt about the graduation that he didn't want to argue with his parents.

Paul shook his head, attempting to clear his mind, as he exited the woogle thicket. He stopped to pluck the half-dozen woogles from his skin. Their little pincers were quite sharp, but it was the only shortcut Paul knew that allowed him to avoid the stomping grounds of the kraken wolves. He would much rather deal with removing a few pesky insects than face off with the oversized wolves.

He sat himself down on an old worn stump and was working away at removing a particularly stubborn woogle attached to his ankle fin, when a large shadow fell over the clearing. The familiar silhouette blocked out much of the moonlight produced by Cascade's twin moons, Gilbert and Sullivan.

"Something eating at you, Paul?" said the dragon, his words rumbling forth not from his mouth, but from his mind.

Paul chuckled with striking insincerity. "You know, if I wanted to be joked to death, I'd have sought out Max."

He stared up at his dragon friend as he discarded the last woogle.

"Ouch. Well, I'll grant you that Max and I share quite a few similarities. We're both gifted with a sense of humor, and..." The dragon snatched a branch topped with leaves and huffed a very warm blast of air at it. The leaves burst into flame.

"Yeah, you're both full of hot air, too," said Paul.

"I was about to say we both help shed light on your troubles, but to each his own, little monster," said Bickyl.

Except for his legs and slender arms, the dragon's scaly body resembled that of a snake. The scrambled mess of horns and spikes that speckled his snout and head, however, destroyed the illusion that Bickyl was just an overgrown snake. The leathery wings, a dragon's pride and joy, made the comparison even less true.

Paul settled on the dragon's shoulder blades where a makeshift saddle had been secured. He laced his feet into the stirrups and grabbed hold of the thick rope that looped around the dragon's midsection. "I could really use a ride."

Bickyl, knowing the pattern of their relationship, replied, "Very well, but someday, you'll have to return the favor."

Paul laughed as the dragon flapped his large wings. The updraft extinguished the flaming branch as the two took to the air.

****

They flew over Cascade in silence for it was rather difficult to hold a conversation astride a flying dragon. The dragon could talk to you with his mind, but the roar of the wind would prevent the dragon from hearing your replies. Bickyl knew Paul was aware of this. Obviously, the monster needed some time to himself, time to gather his thoughts. Being telepathic, dragons appreciate those who nurture their thoughts.

Bickyl coasted higher into the warmer streams of air. Below them, Cascade stretched out in all its majesty. They rode over the Fear Fields, the Monster Academy and even the Oracle Ocean before Bickyl turned about and headed back to the Dragon Reservation. After nearly thirty minutes of flight, Bickyl landed atop a nearby plateau. He sensed Paul was ready to talk.

He quickly lit a fire and curled his tail around to form a tidy resting spot for his monster friend. Paul, paying little attention to the sharp scales of the dragon, snuggled closer to his winged friend.

The fire popped and snapped as it hit air pockets in the wood. A few lava beetles flew to the fire to further investigate its brilliance. Upon feeling the heat radiating from the fire, the beetles grew agitated. Looking for someone to sting in their anger, the insects spied Paul. They also noticed the immense dragon and thought better of launching a stinger attack. They disappeared into the night air, their abdomens glowing a fiery red.

Paul spoke, "You know, they'll glow like that until they sting someone." His voice very mellow.

"Better them than us," said Bickyl.

"Is that a tradition with them?" said Paul.

"No, I think it's an instinct of survival. A lava beetle's sting allows them to get rid of all the poisons in their bodies. They eat just about anything. When you have that kind of appetite, you're bound to eat a few things that aren't healthy. Their sting pushes out the harmful chemicals. It's very cleansing—for them—and very painful for their victims."

"So, they have to get mad to get out the poison, huh?" asked Paul.

The dragon nodded.

"I know someone like that." Paul buried his knuckles in his cheeks. "Goes around tossing out punishments so he doesn't feel so poisoned, I bet."

"Another run-in with your headmaster?"

Paul's lips quivered as he exhaled. "Y-yes."

"Tell me what happened," said Bickyl.

And with the gentle dragon's invite, the floodgates opened up. Paul shared everything that had gone wrong at graduation, the dreadful visit to Stevens's office and the past week of moping around the house. Bickyl listened as the little monster let loose with his frustration and anger. He released his own little pent-up poison. Finally, after Paul had rolled out all the miseries of the past week and held them up to the light for inspection, Bickyl offered advice.

"Traditions are glorious and mighty, Paul. They can also be burdens when abused. The dragons on my reservation remind me of that every day. My father, he wants me to find a treasure trove to guard, to fill the traditional role of a dragon." The dragon placed more wood on the fire with his free hand.

"I'm sorry. I've spent all this time talking about my problems. I forgot to let you share. Are things bad for you?" asked Paul.

"Ah, how thoughtful of you to ask. Actually, our plights have strong similarities. If you would allow me to continue, we might address both our situations," said Bickyl.

Paul rooted through his satchel and produced a poa melon and a brumbleberry sandwich. The sandwich was safely intact. Paul had left Treek at home, as the wormle would've sniffed out the snack and left nothing for the two of them. "Care for some melon?"

"Thank you." Taking the tiny blue melon in his hands, Bickyl speared it with a thin branch and held it over the fire. "I like mine warm," he said, matter-of-factly.

Paul munched on his sandwich, allowing the brumbleberry jelly to ooze. He snatched the excess jelly up with his long tongue, permitting not a drop to fall to the ground. "So, fire away!"

"Truly not a phrase you want to speak to a dragon you aren't chums with, eh?"

Paul frowned.

"Right, the humor thing. You're not in the mood. Got it." The dragon paused to collect his thoughts and pull the melon off his stick. He plopped it into his mouth, and the entire melon disappeared down his throat.

"You really should taste your food," said Paul.

"Yes, well, I'm just so eager to get on with sharing." The dragon again paused. The stars in the night sky twinkled, offering witness and comfort to the confession atop the plateau. "When a dragon reaches adulthood, which I am approaching, he must seek out a treasure. Our tradition dictates we be guardians."

"But you want to be a guardian, right? It's an instinct with you, isn't it?" asked Paul.

"Well, it's more of a tradition. A few dragons have lived their lives quite fully as destroyers."

"But you're not one of those. You wouldn't burn down villages and dash off with helpless damsels, would you?" Paul said, knowingly.

"No, I'm not and I wouldn't. We're not so sure about my cousin Bradley, though. He has pain and fury in his blood," said Bickyl.

Paul recalled his brief encounter with the cousin in question. "No, you're nothing like him."

"In many ways, I am. He too is uncertain how tradition fits into his life. He too seeks a path not offered to him." The dragon shifted his weight, briefly unfurling his wings to stoke the fire. "I just don't see myself sitting atop a mound of gold and jewels, setting fire to anyone foolish enough to steal from me. It doesn't seem very dignified. What good is a treasure that no one gets to see, no one gets to enjoy?"

Paul licked the remaining bits of jelly from his hands. "I bet that's what it's going to be like for me, haunting a pillowcase. I have all this enthusiasm, all this energy for spooking people and I've gotta waste it on such a pathetic job. Heck, even the boy I'm gonna scare has a forgettable name. Barry Busman the Third. What kind of name is that?"

"A name someone treasured enough to pass down from father to son," said Bickyl.

"I graduated with honors. I should be doing more."

"Not every road in your life will be easy to see. You must be a pathfinder."

"What does that mean? Do I take the job? That's not an answer," said Paul. His fins were tinged purple, an obvious physical sign of his growing frustration.

The dragon continued. "My Uncle Frederick, he broke with tradition and yet he managed to keep with tradition."

"How can you do both? I don't understand. Isn't he the uncle the rest of the dragons look down on?"

"Not all of them. Uncle Frederick watches over the son of the god of war. He isn't protecting a pile of gold, but he looks after the boy's welfare. Try telling me he isn't guarding a treasure," said Bickyl.

"So, do you wanna watch over somebody? Is that your path?" asked Paul.

The dragon stood up, being careful to scoop up his friend with his tail. "Who knows? Maybe I've already found my path and I don't know it yet." His amber eyes locked with the little monster's eyes, blazing red from the light of the flames.

"You still haven't told me what I should do. I thought dragons were good at advice." Paul crossed his arms.

"Climb aboard. Let me fly you home. I think we've drained enough poison from your stinger tonight. Tomorrow will bring with it a clear head and maybe a path or two," said Bickyl.

Riddled with doubt, Paul said before the wind drowned out his voice, "Yeah, maybe it'll come to me in a dream."

Behind them, the embers of their fire glowed like the abdomen of a lava beetle.

CHAPTER FIVE
THE ROAD TO RUIN

PAUL SLEPT IN HIS bed without his pillow. The unfortunate bedding lay on the floor, having been torn to pieces earlier in the week during one of Paul's fits of frustration. Paul lay on his mattress with a simple sheet pulled over him. His body twitched, caught up in the spasms of a gripping nightmare.

The dream had started off pleasantly enough, but had soon descended into trouble for the little monster. He was walking down a path with his friends, Max on one side and Bickyl on the other. In front of him, his circus aunts blazed a trail alongside his wormle, Treek, who could talk and crack bad jokes with the rest of them. Everyone except Paul was exchanging jokes he had to admit were fairly funny.

As they walked, the path repeatedly divided. At each fork in the road, one of his friends or family would choose the other path and urge him to proceed onward. After he had waved farewell to both Bickyl and Max, Paul bid goodbye to his pet wormle. Only his aunts remained at his side, but they too soon red. This left Paul all alone to gaze at the path ahead Much like Headmaster Stevens's ceiling, the path red into eager darkness. This filled the lonely monster ad.

was about to step forward when a shadowy figure rose ie darkness lurking before him. Paul could make out e about the stranger, who appeared to be on horseback. loped toward him, Paul soon realized the beast was not se by any stretch of the imagination. The flesh of the ture was festered with black boils, tentacles and menacing ne spurs. The rider of the grotesque mount was even more horrifying. Its bottom heavy, disproportionate legs were wrapped in bandages much like The Flying Mummy. Powerful arms the size of tree trunks hung from the creature's bulging torso, which tugged and pulled at itself as if a nest of snakes slid about underneath the skin. Topping off the monstrosity was a head that was all teeth. Tiny, dark eyes peered out at Paul as if trying to capture him in their stare. The head was framed by a tangled mess of black hair that floated about like the questing tentacles of an octopus. The air seemed thick with decay and ruin as the stranger stepped down from his mount. He approached Paul, his footsteps suspiciously silent. The shadowy stranger kneeled, coming face to face with the dreaming Paul. The little monster fought the urge to run. Every muscle in his body screamed for him to get as far away from the Nightmare Squire as he could.

A questioning look played over Paul's face. *How did I know who he was?*

The Nightmare Squire spoke without moving his lips. The words seemed to fill every nook and cranny in Paul's head as they spilled out. "You know me, little monster. I will soon know you. I have need of you. I need monsters willing to do the job. I need a Grade A spook like yourself…" He laughed and whispered one final word before the dream dissolved into darkness.

PAUL THE PILLOW MONSTER

****

He awakened in a cold sweat, his body trembling. Paul scrambled out of bed, urging his sore muscles to follow a specific course of action. His arms, feeling like lead weights, responded sluggishly as he fumbled to gather up his pillow. His pillow had been one of his most revered heroes, The Flying Mummy. Cascade's tightly wrapped Egyptian hero and leader of The Eternity Guard, the realm's only super-powered protectors, was in sorry shape. Paul retrieved the tattered arms of the mummy from under his bed, located one of the legs and the torso near his nightstand and searched frantically for the head. After scrambling all over the floor for a full minute, he fished the mummy's head and other leg from Treek's glass cage. Treek hissed at his owner for disturbing his slumber. Grabbing the tape from his desk drawer, Paul set forth to repair his pillow. He layered the tape all over the body, laughing uneasily at the notion of bandaging a mummy. Satisfied he had mended his broken hero, Paul returned to his bed, pulled the sheet over himself and clutched the pillow in an iron tight grip of fear. There was no way he would go back to sleep tonight. He would stay awake, with his pillow to watch over him.

Paul fought off the sandman and his gentle charms for most of the night.

Something in his dreams had frightened him. He thought he could place the creature's name, but it was lost in his mind. The name darted in and out of the many hiding places of his subconscious. His nighttime visitor would have to remain nameless for now. Paul could easily recall what the creature had looked like. He also remembered everything the evil thing had said, including the last word the awful stranger had uttered.

Something in his nightmares knew his name.

Near dawn, tired and weak, he drifted off into a dreamless sleep.

****

Deep inside the Dream Mesa, the Nightmare Squire laughed. It was not a laugh laced with joy. It was a laugh filled with pain and madness.

CHAPTER SIX
BREAKFAST OF CHAMPIONS

PAUL PERFORMED HIS DAILY chores in utter silence, appearing withdrawn and slightly dazed. He worried his mother more than usual. Mrs. Palligaster decided to confront her unhappy son. Paul was busy cleaning out the yarka pens when she cornered him.

"Careful, Mom. It's a little slippery in here," warned Paul.

His mother laughed. Her laugh always made Paul's ears tickle. It was one of the sweetest sounds he knew, but it was not enough to rouse him from his funk.

"Paul, dear, perhaps you should take a break. After all, you want to be rested for tonight. You have to haunt Barry Busman. First impressions are so crucial in the fright field, honey." Mrs. Palligaster placed her hand on her son's shoulder. "Why don't you let your brother finish your chores? Go visit Maxwell. I'm sure his quick wit will lift your spirits."

Paul shrugged and resumed shoveling the yarka dung. The

yarka themselves huddled together in the far corner next to the water trough, their caterpillar-shaped bodies bumping into one another in their anxiety at having visitors to their pen.

His mother stood her ground as well as one can stand their ground in a slippery yarka pen. "I insist."

Paul moved his head, barely nodding. He placed the shovel against the side of the pen and hopped over the fence. His mother neatly walked through the pen, avoiding each mound of dung. Exiting from the gate, she smiled warmly at her son.

"Come now, dear. You're acting like Death itself paid you a visit last night." She outstretched her four arms. "You need a hug?"

Paul whistled for Treek, who jumped out of a nearby tree and scampered up onto his shoulder. "No, Mom, I'm okay."

Mrs. Palligaster dropped her arms limply to her side.

Sensing he had wounded his mother, Paul added, "I'll take that hug when I get home, okay?"

Mrs. Palligaster beamed.

Paul disappeared into the grove. He doubted his mother's hug would help ease his troubled mind.

****

Max splashed with great gusto in the tub, although to call it a tub was a disservice. Max's family all ran large, or big boned, his mother liked to say. Their tub occupied roughly the same dimensions as that of a regular swimming pool.

Armed with a wire brush, he scrubbed and scrubbed. The dirt was thick and flaked off with great stubbornness. Max felt the calluses forming on his hands as he gripped the brush even tighter.

"Maxwell, you better be getting rid of that ring in the tub or your father will feed you to the kraken wolves." Mrs. Murble, while not as kindhearted as Paul's mother, was not without her charms.

"Gotcha covered, Mom. I'll have this tub sparkly clean before you can say Flying Mummy," Max shouted down the hall. His mother was in her bedroom, confined to the bed. After the graduation, she had been so stricken with anxiety, she had fallen ill.

Max's father, normally rather chipper and outgoing, had descended into a grump of a mood without his loving wife at his side. The two of them were a rare sight in the fright field, a husband and wife tag team. The couple haunted several antique shops in a reserved small town just outside of Baltimore, Maryland. With his better half sick, he was like a candle without its flame. He mulled around the house all day, bemoaning his misfortune. This only served to further unravel Mrs. Murble.

"What?" said Max's mom.

"Nothing, Mother." Max returned to his chore. He found taking on all the small jobs his mother would normally do helped take his mind off the horrible visitor who had invaded his dreams last night. The shadowy stranger had a name, but Max couldn't think of it. All he remembered were the rows of menacing teeth that overwhelmed the demon's face.

"Maxwell! There's someone at the door. Be a doll and see who it is. If it's that dang talking troll again, send him packing. We don't need any of his miracle medicine. My sister Gladys says he's a charlatan." Amazing that no matter how ill his mother was, her lungs and her volume were never diminished.

Max shambled down the stairs and to the door. He opened it and was immediately set upon by Treek. The furry creature dashed up his chest and clung to his left ear.

Paul stepped in, apologizing. "I'm sorry, Max. I don't know what's gotten into him. He's been acting like this all morning."

"Not a problem."

Both monsters eyed the tiled floor, afraid to meet each other's gaze.

"You doin' okay?" asked Paul.

"Been better. You?" Max pulled Treek off his ear, creating a cradle with his forearms for the wormle to nestle. Treek set upon the new roost with much twittering.

"I'm okay. Little tired. Didn't sleep well last night."

"Me too," said Max. "Must've been one of those nights." Paul nodded.

"Wanna snack?" asked Max.

Paul replied, "Sure. You got any more zackle strips?"

"I think Dad fried some up for breakfast. Let's check." Max shoved off to the kitchen. Paul followed closely behind him, being careful to avoid his friend's large, blue tail.

Max hovered over the stove, inspecting the contents of a large skillet. "Uhm, there's a few strips left, but I gotta warn you, they're a little charred. My dad likes his zackle extra crispy."

Paul grinned. "Same with my dad. I'll take 'em if you've got some holmbread and minotaur milk."

Max produced two slices of holmbread and two mugs of minotaur milk. He pulled out a pair of chairs from the kitchen table, and the friends sat down to breakfast.

"You know, the milk isn't really from the minotaur, right?" said Max, between mouthfuls of holmbread.

"Yeah, I know. You told me this before."

"It can't 'cause the minotaur is male and there's only one of him. He lives in the Shadow Territories last I heard." Max slurped his milk, recklessly spilling the drink across his upper lip and down his chin.

"I know, and the milk really comes from a bunch of cows kept in a maze with no entrance and exit, except for the milkers," said Paul.

"Yeah, the milkers have their own secret entrance and exit. They also have the maze tattooed to their chests in case they get lost. Isn't that cool?" said Max.

"I don't believe the tattoo part. Who'd tattoo a stupid maze to their chest? That's dumb. They just say that on the

Oraclevision to sell more milk. It makes the milk sound mysterious and magical."

Not discouraged by his friend's gloomy mood, Max stood up and deposited his fists against his hips, puffing his chest out to assume the pose of the minotaur from the commercial. He lowered his voice as he parroted the famous bovine. "Start your day right. Grab the bull by the horns. Drink Minotaur Milk."

Paul rolled his eyes.

Max laughed and continued, "This one's my favorite." He flung out his mug toward the imaginary audience. "Minotaur Milk—it's a-maze-ing and that's no bull!"

"Stop it, Max," said Paul.

"What?" Max said, his mug drifting back down to rest on the table.

"Stop pretending that nothing's wrong. Everything's wrong. Today's the day we start our cruddy jobs. I feel like garbage, and you look like someone rolled over you with a steam roller last night, too. Something bad is happening to us." He clutched at his head, rubbing his nest of horns. "Everything's wrong."

Max frowned. "Not everything. We're still friends, right?"

Paul looked up. His jaw dropped slightly as he stared long and hard at Max.

Maxwell Murble gave his friend his goofiest grin.

Paul smiled and laughed. "You're right, everything's not all wrong. We're still friends, you big goof."

CHAPTER SEVEN
BURSTING BUBBLES

IN THE THRONE ROOM of the Dream Mesa, the gloom was thick. The Nightmare Squire reclined sideways on his throne, his attention captured by the images playing across his Conjuring Cobwebs. Each hole in the web held a different scene from all across Cascade. The squire was particularly absorbed in the scene unfolding at the Murble household.

"Oh, bravo!" The King of the Dream Stream clapped his hands together with false enthusiasm. "You can't write sappy lines like that, can you, Swinky?" The squire turned to flash a smile at the gremlin. Armed with a long knitting needle in each paw, Swinky was busy darting around the room, attempting to do battle with a cheery cloud of pink bubbles.

"Yes, I can see the love all over the screen, your royalness." As fast as Swinky popped one of the sugarcoated bubbles, another spilled forth from the out-of-place wishing well tossed off to the side of the throne room.

The Nightmare Squire, ignoring his servant's hyperactive escapades, dwelled on his latest find. "You know, I'm glad I paid those two a visit last night. Experience has taught me those whose dreams are thoroughly squashed make the best Dreamkillers. Am I right, Swinky?"

"Right you are, sir." The gremlin had switched from the large knitting needles to a battle mace. While it was popping more bubbles, it still wasn't taking care of the more perky ones.

"How goes it with killing those daydreams, Swinky? Making decent headway?" asked the Nightmare Squire. Finally, he turned his attention to his servant's task.

More bubbles billowed out of the wishing well as Swinky paused to discuss his options with his boss. "Gotta tell you, Sir Boogeyman, these rascals are near impossible to get rid of."

The King of the Dream Stream waltzed over to his servant and casually took hold of the battle mace. "Please do call me Nightmare Squire only. I detest your obnoxious desire to be creative with my title."

"Righto, Sir Spooks-A-Lot...er...I mean, Nightmare Squire." Swinky paused to scratch his stubby tail. "So, you gonna take care of those daydreams?"

The Nightmare Squire smiled, his teeth gleaming a sickly yellow. "Oh, most definitely. But you were going about it all wrong." He marched over to the wishing well. "If you want to put an end to them, you must get rid of the source." He raised the battle mace high.

"Genius! Pure genius!" squealed the gremlin.

With a thunderous roar, the Nightmare Squire drove the mace deep into the wishing well, crushing its wooden roof and stony walls into splinters and rubble. The floating daydreams crashed to the ground, popping into nothingness.

"I control the Dream Stream!" The Nightmare Squire kicked at the remains of the wishing well. He looked back over at the images of Paul and Max. "And soon, with the help of two foolish monsters, the only threat to my rule will be delivered to my doorstep!"

Throughout the Dream Mesa, the Nightmare Squire's laughter echoed, drowning out all other sounds and fouling the once pure Dream Stream whose rapids ran through the heart of it.

CHAPTER EIGHT
WITH A SIDEWAYS GLANCE

"Not much to look at, is it?" said Max, staring at the dull cliff before them. Small rocks, not even large enough to be deemed boulders, littered the highest point of the cliff. "Nope, isn't very thrilling. Thought it would be flashier."

Paul rolled his eyes at his friend's observations. "You're gonna get us in trouble. Clam up!"

Headmaster Stevens crept up behind them. He had accompanied both young monsters on their first night on the job. "It doesn't have to be showy. That's the idea of Periphery Point."

"Yeah, but shouldn't the entranceway to Earth be dressed up a bit? Maybe some nice boulders with cool engravings depicting monsters past and present making scary faces or something," said Max.

"At least a sign," offered Paul.

"Argh, and to think the two of you graduated with honors!"

The Headmaster pulled at his thinning hair. As he ranted, he waved his arms about willy-nilly. "It's called Periphery Point for a reason. You travel to Earth by going about your task in the most quiet, indirect manner. Otherwise…"

"Otherwise what?" said Max.

"It's in the handbook. As a recent graduate, I would hope you'd know how the gateway between worlds works."

"Of course we do. I'm just seeing if what you said back at your office was the truth. If you've memorized the handbook, you'd know the answer," said Max, crossing his arms.

Paul tugged at Max's tail. "What are you doing?"

"Just having a little fun. What's he gonna do? Get us worse jobs than we already have?"

"The two of you bring shame to the academy's good name," said the headmaster. "You don't deserve to spook anyone."

"Oh, I don't know. We seem to be doing a good job at rattling your chain," said Max. "C'mon, Headmaster, tell us or we'll quit."

"What?" said Paul.

Headmaster Stevens stared at Max. One could just imagine steam pouring forth from his ears.

Paul tugged at his friend's ear, pulling the giant closer to chew him out. "Have you lost your mind? What are you doing?"

"Trust me. I'm just pushing back a little. You know we got a raw deal. Let me play with the creep a little," said Max, plastering a pout across his face.

Paul huffed and turned away, kicking at the puny rocks at his feet.

"How dare you…" began the headmaster.

Max held his hand to silence the elder. "Hush. I think it's time you listened to me. Tell us about Periphery Point or we quit, and there goes your 100% placement record."

"What? No…" The headmaster fumed, pondering his predicament.

"We're waiting, sir," said Max.

The headmaster wagged a finger at the two monsters, while stammering out his answer. "If I do, will you please just do your jobs?"

"Let me confer with my associate. Excuse me." Max whirled around and slunk over to Paul.

"This is so dumb," said Paul.

"Shhh. Don't show him a shred of weakness." Switching his voice to a knowing tone just loud enough for the headmaster to hear, Max blathered on. "I don't know, he's offering us a pretty good deal. If you wanna hold out for three weeks of vacation and a Christmas bonus, who am I to argue?"

Paul squawked. Max covered his mouth.

"Just kidding." He flashed a toothy, then plodded back over to the headmaster. "Well, we've discussed your offer and we agree to live by the terms."

The headmaster stomped at the ground before rolling his eyes back as if to read off his answer from the inside of his skull. "Periphery Point exists in all places and no place at once. It is a gateway powered by ignorance and nonsense. Fright teams or individuals may access Earth using Periphery Point by simply standing on its unassuming apex and making a sideways look without moving one's head. This weak attempt to glance at the images dancing at the corners of our eyes opens the door and spills forth any and all magical creatures inhabiting a three-foot radius into the connecting world or dimension. Fueled by the belief that one has seen something distressing at the periphery of their vision, Periphery Point is one of the most magical, yet mundanely bland, areas of Cascade.

"Rumors abound about its creation, but academy elders strongly suspect the Wizard Bailey and three other lesser known wizards were instrumental in its creation." The headmaster rolled his eyes back down to deliver a piercing look at Max.

Max waved his hands loosely in front of him. "Wheew!

Now that was impressive. You even cited the footnote about the Wizard Bailey."

"Yes, well, yea for me. Now, get going. Your sock drawer and Paul's pillow await." The headmaster brushed imaginary dust from his sleeves.

Paul stepped up and peered closely at Max in a new light.

"What's that look for?" said Max defensively. "I don't think I like that look."

"Oh, it's nothing. I just didn't know you had so much poison to get out of your system." Paul bowed politely at the headmaster and made his way to the highest stretch of ground on Periphery Point.

Max shot Stevens one last look. "Now when you say apex, you mean the tippy top, right?" He hustled over to his friend.

Paul looked up at Max. "You ready?" he asked.

"Ready as I'll ever be. Sure hope the kid's socks don't stink."

Paul giggled. "I'll tell you about mine if you tell me yours when we get back."

"Deal," said Max. As an afterthought, he added, "You gotta fill me in on that poison comment. I didn't quite get it."

Paul glanced sideways, attempting to trap the shadows that danced just out of reach in his gaze. "Oh, I'll tell you all about that and lava beetles, too. You're never gonna look at them the same."

Max scratched his head as he watched Paul disappear into nothingness. The big blue monster shot a hasty glance sideways and found himself whisked away to Earth.

Headmaster Stevens, satisfied the two had left the scene, turned and made his way back down the mountain and to the safety of his office in the academy. At least there he would be safe from the biting stings of the lava beetles that roamed all over Cascade. He had been stung twice while standing on Periphery Point. Even during his childhood, the ferocious lava beetles had always singled him out as a perfect victim. His

PAUL THE PILLOW MONSTER

mother attributed it to him being so sweet, but even the headmaster doubted that hypothesis.

CHAPTER NINE
SEEING STARS

Paul landed atop a rather pointy item in the closet of Barry Busman. He looked down to see he sat perched on a ramshackle pile of action figures. The pointy toy demanding his attention looked like a robotic cheetah with large missiles mounted over each shoulder. The left missile was jabbing him in the side. Paul hopped down off the pile, landing on a tangled mess of scarves and sweaters. He peered out the cracks of the closet door to see that Barry's room was indeed vacant of any human. The spell that shuffled them from Cascade to Earth was very selective about when it deposited a monster in their haunting spot. It never materialized them in a room occupied by people. Paul had fretted that it would, but was pleased to see the magic was working correctly.

He was about to push open the closet door when a voice that sounded like a concrete mixer on overdrive bellowed from the far corner of the closet.

"So you the new guy, huh?" From behind a storage box of building blocks, a squat, four-footed monster with fancy gills along the sides of its face stepped out. The yellow creature was speckled with bright purple dots.

"Um, hi...I'm Paul."

The closet monster eyed him suspiciously. "You're a first timer, aren't you?"

Paul said, "Uhm, yes. I..."

"You look familiar. What's your full name?" The yellow monster dragged three tails behind him. Each was decorated with a single blue star at the end.

"Paul Phineas Palligaster."

"I knew it. You're Conrad's boy, aren't you?" said the closet monster.

"That's my dad, right. Who are you? I don't think I've ever seen you around the house." Paul now eyed him suspiciously.

"Stargon Stackle," he said.

"Pleased to meet you, Stargon." Paul bowed.

"Bah, stop that. Always hated that bowing garbage. So stuffy." Stargon pawed at the sweaters and scarves, attempting to straighten them up. Paul noticed that the sleeves of each sweater were tied to the scarves forming a long coiled clothing chain. "Call me Starry, okay?"

Paul smiled. "Okay, Starry."

Starry flashed a pleasant smile, revealing row upon row of fine, very sharp teeth.

Paul looked out the slits in the closet door. "Wow, two monsters assigned to one kid. This Barry Busman must be some nasty to deserve so much scaring. Since this is your home turf, you got any surefire scare tactics?"

"Nope. In fact, I have only one rule and you better stick to it," said Starry.

Paul leaned forward.

Starry glared at him. "Don't bother the kid."

Paul shrunk back, his eyes widening in disbelief. "I don't

understand. What do you mean don't bother the kid?"

Starry growled and thrashed his three tails. The stars at the end of each tail looked extremely pointy and sharp. "The kid's got enough things going wrong in his life. He doesn't need us mucking it up further. Got it?"

"But that's our job..." Paul squeaked out.

"No, that's not our job, not always. Did you read your handbook or what?" Starry licked his front paws thoughtfully.

"Ummm..." Paul said.

"It's all spelled out for you in Chapter 12: What to do with a child facing emotional hardships. Don't you remember that?" Starry had quietly knotted a rather large purple sweater to the clothing chain and was now attempting to add a fuzzy green garment to the mix.

"Umm, there's no Chapter 12 in the handbook," Paul said.

"What?"

"There are only ten chapters." Paul felt very uncomfortable. Perhaps Starry's age also affected his memory.

"Gadzooks, what kind of academy is Headmaster Steamhoover running there? He's taken out the two most important chapters." Clearly upset, Starry tossed the green sweater aside and pressed even closer toward Paul.

Paul backed away from the closet monster. "Headmaster Steamhoover? Who's he? Stevens is our headmaster. How long has it been since you've been back to Cascade?" asked Paul.

"I don't know. Twenty years or so," said Starry.

"Oh my," said Paul.

"Shhhh," hissed Starry. "Barry's coming, and it sounds like he's crying again."

Paul whimpered as the door to the bedroom burst open. Paul squealed as the boy ripped open the closet door and crumpled to the floor. The boy's head fell only inches from Starry. Paul backed up, searching for something to hide under.

"Oh, Starry, they're at it again. They came back all fired up." Barry sobbed, not even looking up as he talked.

PAUL THE PILLOW MONSTER

What is going on here? Paul thought as the missile-wielding cheetah robot fell on him, causing him to blast out a scream.

CHAPTER TEN
OF SCARVES AND SCARES

LETTING ONESELF BE SEEN by a child was a true crime. Monsters should be heard and felt, but never seen. It should be up to the child's imagination to create their own terrifying image of what haunted them. Paul had broken the ultimate rule of frightening on his first visit. He wrestled with the silly cheetah toy that had landed on him as he attempted to dive deeper into the closet and away from the wide-eyed stare of Barry Busman.

"Relax, kiddo. Barry's not gonna hurt you," said Starry.

"He's not supposed to see us," stammered Paul as he tossed the robot cheetah off to his left.

Barry pushed aside a container of Lincoln Logs to better examine his newest visitor. "Wow, a second monster? They sent me a second monster, Starry. Why'd they do that?"

Paul's jaw dropped. "He knows you? You've let him see you!" Paul swung an accusing finger at the elder monster.

"That is so not good."

Barry extended his right hand to shake Paul's, not flinching in fear one bit. "I'm Barry. What's your name and specialty?"

"Umm..." Paul stared in horror at the little boy. Barry was a tiny child with a big bushy head of black hair. A tiny button nose was situated at the center of his face above a smile that was small, but full of warmth. Outside of the tears that streaked down his cheeks, he looked altogether quite cheery. Paul remembered from reading the boy's file that he was nine years old and causing a great deal of trouble acting out in school. He hardly looked the type to cause anyone difficulty.

Starry glanced at Paul with a pleading look. "His name is Paul. He's my assistant. His specialty is finding lost souls."

Paul wrinkled his nose. "What?"

Starry scampered over to Paul, faster than his old bones looked like they could travel. Starry whispered in Paul's ear, "Play along, and I'll fill you in later."

"But he's seen us! We're in so much hot water. I don't..." said Paul.

Starry squeezed Paul's right arm. Through clenched teeth, he hissed, "Just play along!"

Paul swallowed hard. Starry's eyes flashed red with intensity. He had never heard of another monster attacking a fellow fright fiend, but didn't want to risk it. "Okay, I'll calm down."

"Good," said Starry.

"Is he okay? Did I say something wrong?" said Barry, his eyes retreating inward as if he was ashamed of extending a warm greeting. The child pulled back his hand, cradling it in his lap.

Starry jumped aboard the boy's nest of hair and flicked his tail about like a child's mobile. The stars mounted on his tails glowed a bright yellow. "Not at all. Paul's just a little new to his job and not the most well-mannered beast. Please forgive him, Barry."

Barry seemed to perk up at the explanation. Soon, he was chattering away at Paul. "Are you really good at finding lost souls? Starry said he can do it, but I bet we'll find him in no time with your help." Barry snaked out his open hand again and Paul shook it reluctantly. Barry sprang to his feet, nearly pulling up Paul with his sudden movement.

Paul pulled his hand back to his side, nursing it in amazement with his other hand. He had actually touched a child. What other horrible thing would happen to him next?

Barry bolted to his bed. Starry trotted out of the closet. Turning to face Paul, he whispered, "Get out here. Tonight's an important night."

Barry was on his bed, stuffing several pairs of pants in a large duffel bag. "I've got everything I'll need for the journey: flashlight, snacks, thermos, matches, twenty dollars and my yo-yo. We're gonna find him, and then he'll never leave again."

Paul shot Starry a questioning look.

Starry ignored Paul and directed the boy. "Now remember, this is only an overnight trip. If we don't find him tonight, we'll look again tomorrow night. I don't think you'll need that many pants."

Barry smiled at Starry as he removed the pants. "Okay, but…"

"No buts. This is only an overnight trip. I will not have your parents worrying about you if we don't arrive back before morning."

Barry's enthusiasm died slightly. "Foster parents," he uttered.

"Barry, they care about you. They do. They are just going through a selfish time in their lives. Ease up on them. Let them sort out their troubles." Starry's voice stayed evenly measured.

"O-kay," replied Barry.

Starry disappeared back into the closet and returned dragging the chain of knotted scarves and sweaters.

Barry had hopped over to the windowsill and was waving at Paul. "C'mon, Paul. We don't have a lot of time." The tiny boy struggled to push open the window. It opened slowly.

Paul glanced at the older monster to see he was busy tying one end of the clothing chain to a sturdy wooden bedpost. Paul watched as Starry, satisfied with the double knot he had tied, leaped over to the windowsill, the end scarf of the chain secure in his mouth.

Paul inched toward the window. They were on the second floor. The scarves were obviously a crude rope. Paul said, "Hey, we can't leave the room. That's not in the handbook."

Starry snarled at him.

Barry frowned. "Please, you gotta help me."

Paul made a split decision. He had had enough of this nonsense. He was going to return to Cascade and file a report about Starry and the whole mess. He slid his eyes to the right, attempting to glance again at the shadows that danced at the corners of his vision. Starry saw what he was doing and yelled, "No, don't! You're too close to…"

His protest came too late. Barry's bedroom filled with light as Paul's sideways glance triggered the gate.

CHAPTER ELEVEN
PUT A SOCK IN IT

MAX SAT ATOP THE tallest rock on Periphery Point. Sadly, the rock measured no more than two feet in height. Max had hoped for a more proper, dignified perch like a large whale-sized boulder, but the small stone he sat upon had the best view of the woods leading to the point. He could keep an eye out for Headmaster Stevens if he returned to check on them. He also had a clear shot of where his friend would be returning from Earth. Max had returned to Cascade, tumbling onto the rock-strewn ground of the cliff only minutes after leaving. He had chickened out of actually doing his job. Inhabiting a sock drawer and being terrifying with footwear seemed an impossible feat. Max had simply decided to avoid it. As soon as he had plopped down in his victim's empty bedroom, Max had done a quick inspection of the girl's surroundings. Finding very little of interest and his mind distracted by his frustration at such a lowly job, Max had chosen to return to Cascade

PAUL THE PILLOW MONSTER

slightly ahead of schedule.

Max had been prepared to wait the whole night for Paul to return. Paul, as much as Max knew his friend disliked his assignment, played by the rules. He would stay the whole night in his depressing position as a pillow monster. Imagine Max's surprise when Paul spilled forth from the gate a mere five minutes after himself. Imagine Max's utter shock at the hitchhikers Paul brought back to Periphery Point.

Dropping out of the gate in the air was not only his scaly orange friend, but also a yellow creature with a trio of star-tipped tails and a small boy dressed in brown shorts and a simple white T-shirt with a large duffel bag in tow.

Max rushed over to Paul's side. "What are you doing? You brought back hitchhikers!"

Paul rubbed his head. The return trip had not been pleasant. His head throbbed from the small stone that his forehead had landed upon. He shook his head to clear the cobwebs from his mind, but was greeted with simply more pain. "Oww, that hurts," he mumbled.

Paul rose to his feet and steadied himself by gripping Max's huge forearms. He looked back to see Starry and Barry rising, both equally dazed and confused.

Max yelled, uncertain his friend had heard him, "You brought somebody back! Are you nuts?"

Paul wobbled. "Please, stop yelling. My head is really woozy."

Starry, seeming fully recovered from the disorienting trip, scampered up to the two monsters. "Hate to spoil your reunion, boys, but we've got a major problem."

Barry said, "Starry, Paul, where are we? Why are there two moons?"

Max puffed out a blast of air. "He knows your name? The human knows you?"

Barry, finally noticing Max, said, "Wow, another monster. This is great! We're gonna be the best search party!"

61

Starry ordered the boy to sit down. "I'll fill you in on our whereabouts in a minute, Barry. Why don't you make sure you brought everything, okay?"

Barry, happy to take orders from his trusted monster, unzipped his duffel bag to inventory the contents.

Starry turned to face Max and Paul. He directed his pointed comments at the smaller of the two. "You can't bring a boy back here! That's just not done!"

Paul said, "Well, you should know about breaking rules, huh?"

Max looked back and forth as the anger erupted from both monsters. "I know my place. It is entirely proper to assist mortal children. If you look in…"

"I don't care about what your handbook with the stupid missing chapter says. Just put a sock in it!" screamed Paul at Starry.

Max stepped back. Paul very rarely lost his temper. His friend was raving at the older monster with little concern for the hurt his words possessed. "Paul, you shouldn't talk to an elder monster like that," said Max.

Paul whirled to stare down his friend. "Don't even, Max. Not after how you acted with Headmaster Stevens. Just…" Paul looked like he was about to explode. "Just don't." His voice dropped an octave, sounding as if it had lost its way.

Starry's voice changed as well. It conveyed concern. "Paul, we all need to calm down. You're right. This situation goes beyond the handbook, but it doesn't go beyond our duties." He shook a tail toward Barry. "We have a boy who needs us."

Paul nodded. Max frowned. He had no idea what was going on and even less confidence that his friend knew what he was doing. Following Starry's lead, Max struck a different tone with what he said next. "What can I do?"

Paul sat down on a toadstool whose height would make most of the rocks on Periphery Point green with envy. "I don't know. Maybe Starry knows what we should do."

Starry said, "Barry shouldn't be here. We need to get him back to Earth."

Paul and Max nodded.

The trio of monsters was about to put their plan into action when a voice dripping with windswept wisdom filled the clearing. "The boy's quest lies in Cascade."

All turned to see a wizard emerge from the woods, and, with his robes trailing in the air, the ancient spellcaster floated over to face them.

Paul recognized immediately who their magical guest was. "The Wizard Bailey!"

CHAPTER TWELVE
A WELL-TIMED WIZARD

THE LARGE GAUNTLETS THAT covered the wizard's forearms glowed yellow, bursting with magic. As the Wizard Bailey levitated toward them, Paul saw why his feet didn't touch the ground. The wizard was rather short, probably no more than four feet in stature. By hovering above the ground, he rose up above even Max in height. Paul looked up at the wizard. Eyes brimming with power sat deeply underneath large, fluffy eyebrows. Equally noticeable was the matching mustache that appeared bushy and full under the new arrival's slightly upturned nose. Paul could not tell if the wizard's hair matched his silver eyebrows and mustache, as his head was covered in a skin-tight skullcap with long, flowing flaps that circled around the back of the wizard's head.

The wizard never took his eyes off Paul. "Barry's quest is here in Cascade."

Max stood speechless.

Starry, however, glared at the wizard with mistrust. "Wizards are all blowhards. They talk in riddles and offer promises stolen from dreams."

At the mention of dreams, the wizard took his eyes off Paul and stared at the older monster. "Wise words, Starry."

Starry, not the least bit disturbed that the wizard knew his name, said, "Why are you here, Wizard?"

"For the same reason as you." He gestured an open, inviting hand toward Barry who had stopped examining his duffel bag and stood, staring at the wizard, his mouth agape. The wizard returned his eyes to Paul.

"Hmph. Pretty convenient appearance, you showing up here," said Starry.

"I could mutter about destiny and fate, but I doubt that would persuade you," said the Wizard Bailey. "Instead, I'll appeal to a clear head."

The wizard gestured with his right hand. Shimmering snowflakes of fire danced forth from his gauntlet, gathering together to form a cobweb in the air. "Conjure thee a view of hope above this starry slope." Twinkling into life in the cobweb was a scene that sparked Barry to cry in joy.

"Spence! He's here! Look!" The boy reached for the magical web, hoping to pull it and the image of his brother closer.

Paul peered at the web. A boy, looking much like Barry, but taller and with black glasses, sat on the shore of a small island. Black waves lapped at the sand around him. The boy's face held an expression of sadness.

Barry grabbed Starry by his tails and twirled him in the air. The monster protested weakly. "Barry, please. Put me down."

"He's here. We have to get to him." Barry danced lightly atop Periphery Point.

The Wizard Bailey smiled widely.

Paul said, "I can't tell where he is."

The Wizard Bailey waved the spell away, urging the web to

evaporate into the night. "You must travel to the Dream Mesa. Your brother needs your help. You must go there next."

Max and Paul flinched. They knew who called the Dream Mesa home. The name that had escaped them all morning, clawed its way to the surface. In unison, they said, "The Nightmare Squire!"

CHAPTER THIRTEEN
SPELLING TROUBLE

PAUL AND MAX LOOKED at Barry Busman. The boy stood before them with his hands open, palms facing upward as he kneeled down. "Please, you have to go. We need your help," said Barry, casting his large eyes unavoidably in their direction.

Starry sat with his back to the threesome. Dawn was streaking the Cascade sky with its warm urgings of oranges and yellows.

Max looked at Paul. "What do we do? We can't take him back now. Periphery Point works best at night, and we couldn't even get it to work then." After the wizard's departure, Paul and Starry had gotten into another large argument. The result was a waste of most of the night thanks to their mutual stubbornness. Paul felt that the next step was to follow the quest encouraged by the Wizard Bailey. Starry, uneasy about the spellcaster, wanted them to return Barry to Earth. Around midnight, Paul had agreed to return Barry to his room until they checked out the wizard's story further. But upon trying to summon a gate, they found they couldn't. No matter how many sideways glances each of the three monsters tried, they couldn't return the boy to safety that night.

Barry Busman was stranded in Cascade.

"I think we can only visit Earth once each night. We'll have to wait till tomorrow night to return him," said Paul.

"I think I remember that from the handbook," said Max.

"It is from the handbook. This isn't good," said Starry. "His parents will surely panic when they don't find him under the covers. I imagine they are waking up about now." Starry shuddered.

"This must be a sign. We have to take him to the Dream Mesa," said Paul.

Max could tell his little friend said these words with an undercurrent of fear. During the course of the night, both had shared their disturbing dreams with each other and were not eager to meet up with the unnamed stranger they now knew to be the Nightmare Squire.

"Why are you being such a cheerleader for visiting the mesa?" asked Max. "He's the ruler there, you know."

Paul said, "I know. I don't want to go there any more than you do, but something is pushing us in that direction."

"I thought we didn't like to be pushed around," said Max.

Paul smiled. "We don't, but this seems important, like we're supposed to do this, doesn't it?"

Max left the question unanswered, for coming out of the woods at that moment was Headmaster Stevens. Starry grabbed Barry and retreated along with Max and Paul to the relative hiding place of a nearby brumbleberry tree.

Headmaster Stevens stood at the highest point on the cliff and looked around. He closed his eyes, faced the rising sun and began muttering in a language that none recognized. Upon uttering his last word, the air around the point shimmered and hiccupped. Satisfied he had done his appointed job, Stevens retreated to the woods.

Periphery Point was disturbingly quiet.

Paul whispered, "What did he do? I didn't understand the words he used except for my name and Max's."

Max said, "It sounded like a spell. I didn't know Stevens did magic."

"It was a spell, and he shouldn't know how to cast a spell," said Starry.

"You knew what he was saying?" asked Paul.

"Yes," said Starry. "He just closed the gates to and from Cascade for you and Max. He thinks he's trapped you on Earth."

Paul and Max whimpered as they tried to hold back their fear.

CHAPTER FOURTEEN
HEAD OF STEAM

IN ITALY, ALL ROADS supposedly lead to Rome. For Paul and Max, every pathway around them seemed to be closing off and leading them in one distinct direction—The Dream Mesa.

"How can he do magic?" said Max. "That's impossible! Monsters can't work magic." The band of adventurers had left Periphery Point and were mulling about the forest near Paul's house, uncertain of their next move.

Barry, eager to rescue his brother, played like a broken record with his pleas. "Why are we waiting around here? I thought we were going to get Spence."

It took all of Starry's energy to keep the boy in their unusual camp, a large brumbleberry tree. Paul and Max had hollowed out the bottom to make a fort when they were much younger. Inside the still living tree, they had decorated their secret hideout with Flying Mummy posters and cutouts from their hero's official comic book.

Max stood in the tree's entryway, keeping guard. "We need time to think," said Max.

"Maybe your headmaster is more than meets the eye," said Starry.

"What do you mean?" asked Paul.

"If monsters don't do magic, then maybe your beloved headmaster is not one of us," suggested Starry.

"He is not beloved, believe me," muttered Max.

"He's our headmaster. He's in charge. He has to be a monster. Wouldn't the other staff sniff him out if he wasn't a fellow monster?" asked Paul.

"I don't have the answers," said Starry. "I'm only guessing."

"Well, no matter what he is, we certainly can't return to the academy. It's obvious we're not welcome there," said Paul.

"It's odd you've never heard of Headmaster Steamhoover," said Starry. "You sure his name doesn't ring a bell? For either of you?"

Max and Paul shook their heads.

Max said, "Before Headmaster Stevens took over the school about twenty years ago, his father ran the place for like forever. I think my dad went to school under him."

"My dad did, too. He's always telling me how Headmaster Stevens is just as grumpy as his father was." Paul handed Barry a Flying Mummy comic and urged him to read it.

"That's also odd. If his father was headmaster before him, I would know. I went to school with both your fathers. We graduated together. Your father was our valedictorian. He got into an argument with the podium dragon and Headmaster Steamhoover had to step in." Starry seemed caught up in remembering the scene. His eyes glazed over.

"That's not possible. Headmaster Stevens the First was at my father's graduation." Paul's head was beginning to hurt.

"Well, I suspect a spell might be at work here," said Starry.

"What kind of spell?" asked Paul.

"I don't know, but I have this feeling that our headmaster

mystery and the missing chapters of the handbook are related," said Starry.

"Ha! I can solve that!" said Max. The large monster reached a massive paw into a very tall alcove cut into the tree. "I have an extra copy of the handbook here!"

Starry and Paul glanced nervously at each other.

Max pulled down a tattered edition of *The Monster's Handbook*.

"It's a paperback!" said Starry, surprise coloring his voice.

"Of course it is. My hardbound copy is at home. I wouldn't keep that one in this old tree. Too expensive."

"We never had a paperback version of the handbook. Steamhoover was against printing it in that form. He was all about tradition." Starry snatched the book from Max.

"Be careful of my bookmark. It's a collector's edition battle bookmark," said Max.

Starry flipped through the book in a crazed manner, his eyes growing wider as he approached the end of the book. "The last two chapters are missing."

Max and Paul folded their arms. "There are only ten chapters. It's the same as the hardbound edition," said Paul.

Starry dropped the book to the ground. "This isn't right. Not right at all."

His nervous breakdown was interrupted by a squeal of fear from Barry. "Eeeeya!"

The trio of monsters turned to see what was wrong. Barry huddled against the interior of the tree farthest from the entrance, his small hands waving helter-skelter as the boy looked to the outside. "Um, big…dragon…out…there."

The snout of Bickyl the Dragon pushed its way into the tree. Puffs of smoke curled up from the dragon's nostrils, only inches away from Barry. "Hi, guys, what's up?" The dragon's words echoed through their minds.

CHAPTER FIFTEEN
TIPPING THE SCALES

THE SCALES ON THE dragon's forehead were the softest point on his head. The winged serpent purred pleasantly as Paul scratched the beast's hide.

"See? He's a friendly dragon," said Paul, holding the boy up to his friend. "Bickyl wouldn't hurt a fly."

"Not true. If a fly stood between me and a ripe melon, an insect swatting might be in order." The dragon thumped his tail to punctuate his sentence.

"Your voice in my head tingles," said Barry.

Barry was attempting to swing his leg over the dragon's snout as if it were a saddle. Bickyl lowered his head so the boy could hop on. Barry giggled as he rocked about on his new ride.

The dragon chuckled. "I can't say I've been around any mortals before, but he's fun."

"Why are you here? I don't think you've ever left the

reservation before," said Paul.

The dragon's eyelids drooped. "It wasn't by choice. My father gave me an ultimatum."

"What?" said Paul.

The dragon pulled his head out of the tree cave, being careful with his enthusiastic cargo. "He told me to leave and not come back unless I'd found my own treasure trove to guard."

"You can't go home?" asked Barry.

"No, little one, not until I find my place," said Bickyl.

"You should come with us," said Barry.

"And where are you going?" The dragon eyed the ripe brumbleberries clustered in the high branches above him. He licked his lips, his tongue tickling Barry in the process.

Paul quickly explained everything that had happened to them. Bickyl listened intently. "…and we were just looking at the handbook when you arrived." Paul rubbed the neck of the dragon as he finished his tale.

"It sounds like you've got yourself a quest." Bickyl slowly rose, bringing his head up to the closest cluster of brumbleberries. His tongue snaked out to snatch the berries from their haven. "Care for another tag-along?"

"But what about your treasure?" asked Paul. "Your dad…"

"That can wait. Your troubles sound a bit more urgent than me finding a pile of gold and rubies to make my mattress," Bickyl smiled.

Paul's confidence was boosted by the dragon's participation.

"Awesome! We should make it to the Dream Mesa in no time flat with you as our ride," said Max.

The dragon blew a warm blast of air at Max. "Don't be silly, Max. I couldn't possibly carry all of you. You'd be too heavy."

"Oh," said Max, disappointed he would not be experiencing his first flight atop a dragon.

"I can certainly act as a scout though. Fly ahead and check

things out, you know." Bickyl flapped his wings confidently.

Starry asked, "You do have a map of Cascade, don't you?"

Max smiled. "Of course we do. Let me go get it." He disappeared into the tree hideout for a minute and returned with a tattered and incorrectly folded map. "Next stop, the Dream Mesa!"

Paul, along with Max, Starry and a small mortal boy dragging a tidy, yet large, duffel bag, scurried into the woods as the dragon took to the air.

****

Emerging from a thicket behind the secret hideout, Headmaster Stevens watched them set forth. He hunched over and deposited Treek on the ground. Paul's pet blinked its eyes forcefully, attempting to erase the hypnotic spell the headmaster had directed at him.

"Go, silly creature. Meet up with your owner and be my eyes and ears."

Treek, eager to put as much distance between him and the unpleasant man, hopped into the woods after Paul. Headmaster Stevens melted back into the woods, sparing hardly a glare at his new puppet.

CHAPTER SIXTEEN
IDOL CHATTER

THE TRIP THROUGH THE Forever Forest did indeed feel like it took a good amount of time. It was noon before they took a break. Starry insisted they take a rest.

"I can't believe Treek found me," said Paul as they cupped their hands and drank from the spring Starry had located. Treek was curled around Paul's neck, snuggling affectionately against his owner.

Treek had pounced on them moments after they had left the tree hideout. Barry had been instantly attracted to the strange pet. Oddly enough, Treek wanted nothing to do with the mortal. Paul assured the boy that Treek would warm up to him.

"Little beast has quite a sense of direction," said Max, splashing his friend. Treek uncoiled just enough to properly hiss at the larger monster for the soaking.

"Shame you have no such quality," said Starry to Max. "When does your glorious map say this forest should end?"

Max eyed the map, holding it away from the probing eyes of the older monster. "Another mile or so and we'll be out of this forest and into the Screaming Plains."

"Oh, they sound lovely. Given any thought to their naming?" asked Starry.

"Nope," said Max. "But you'll probably feel right at home what with all the moaning you do."

Paul deposited Treek on a mound of hushrooms and walked over to Barry. Treek devoured them in complete silence. Even his belches were muted thanks to the magic of the hushrooms.

Barry was sitting on a log, playing with his yo-yo. "I wish I'd packed a sandwich or something."

Paul motioned for him to stand. "Come on. I have just the feast for you."

Paul ran to the base of a large tree whose bark was a rich purple. He pulled free a long strip of bark and set forth chewing on it. He peeled off a second piece and handed it to Barry. "Here, have some."

The boy eyed the food with uncertainty.

"C'mon, it's just tree taffy. Give it a try."

Barry inched his mouth toward the bark. He tugged at with his fingers, attempting to pull off a small piece to sample. "Hey, it's sticky."

"That's why we call it taffy." Paul had finished his first strip and was busy removing a second helping.

Barry nudged a small piece of the bark into his mouth. He chewed it slowly. "It tastes like taffy flavored jerky." Barry pushed a larger piece in his mouth. "It's pretty good."

They sat on a nearby stump and gulped down three strips each before Paul asked Barry about his brother. "Your brother is missing?"

Barry stopped eating and fidgeted with the last strip of tree taffy. He rubbed at the frayed ends of the taffy with a thumb and forefinger. "Yeah, he went to bed one night and the next morning my parents wouldn't let me go see him. They said he ran away."

"Oh," said Paul. "How long ago?"

"Three years," said Barry, tossing the remaining bark to the ground.

"Spence hated being in foster care. He was convinced our parents were still alive and wanted to see us," said Barry.

"What are foster parents?"

"They are parents who help out when your real parents... don't want you anymore."

Paul stopped chewing on his taffy. *How could parents be so cruel?* he thought. He sat next to Barry, uncertain how to respond.

"Spence and I have always been together. The Hollinsmiths are our second foster parents," said Barry.

Paul listened.

"They try to be good, but after Spence disappeared, they began to fight a lot." Barry's voice fluttered. "I think they're gonna get a divorce."

"What happens to you then?" asked Paul.

"Another foster family lets me stay with them." Barry rubbed his eyes.

Paul shifted the conversation. "What is your brother like?"

Barry cheered up at this question. "Spence is incredible. He can draw almost anything and he's the coolest skateboarder. He was gonna teach me how to do a nosegrind right before he left."

"That sounds painful."

Barry laughed. "He also helped me with school. He got me writing stories, really fun stories. My teacher really liked them."

"Sounds like a good big brother," said Paul.

"He is."

Paul and Barry sat together in silence. The young monster felt unsure of what to say next. Luckily, he didn't have to worry. Max burst onto the scene with major news.

"Guys, Bickyl just flew back and said we're only about half

a mile away from the Screaming Plains."

"Oh," said Paul, confused about how to proceed with Barry.

"Let's get going. I bet we can cross the plains before it gets too dark." Max grabbed Barry's duffel bag. "I'll carry the kid's bag for a while. C'mon."

The adventurers, encouraged to hear the Forever Forest did not live up to its name, resumed their quest. In the back of Starry's mind, he tried to remember the meaning behind the Screaming Plains. Unfortunately, his time away from Cascade had dulled his memory.

How terrible could the place be if he couldn't recall any dangers associated with it?

CHAPTER SEVENTEEN
SEEING RED

OTHER THAN MAX BEING chased by a small swarm of lava beetles, the final trek through the Forever Forest proved uneventful. As the vegetation began to thin ahead of them, they could make out the flat, barren landscape of the Screaming Plains.

With the dragon flying high overhead, the three monsters and Barry stepped out of the woods and onto the plains. Other than a few oddly stacked boulders dotting the horizon, the plains were quite stark. The ground beneath them was colored a deep red.

Barry fell to his knees and pushed his fingers into the scarlet soil. "It's really squishy."

Max placed his right foot onto the soft ground. It sank nearly a foot. "You don't sink too far. Feels firm enough."

Starry and Paul, much shorter than their large friend, frowned.

Starry scowled, "Speak for yourself. That stuff's pretty deep."

"It's not gonna be like quicksand, is it?" asked Barry.

Paul stepped into the soft soil. He sank up to his knees. "I don't think so. Max is right. The ground underneath seems pretty solid." Paul took half a dozen steps further into the red landscape.

Max smiled. "I can carry everybody on my shoulders if that'll make you feel better." He sent a lingering look toward Starry.

Starry sucked in his lower lip, thinking about his options. "You'll go slowly and check for any sudden drop-offs?"

Max nodded. "Most definitely."

Starry looked at Paul.

"You and Barry should ride on Max. I'll try wading through this stuff with him. That way, we can be twice as certain of solid footing," said Paul.

Just then, Bickyl landed in the clearing, on an open spot not covered in the red soil. "It isn't far. The plain only extends for about two miles."

Paul asked, "Do you know if it's dangerous?"

"No. I have not traveled this far from the reservation and I don't recall anyone telling me why these plains scream. I don't hear any shouting." Bickyl slid his tail into the soil. "Actually, it feels quite warm. I don't think you're in any danger."

Starry scrambled onto Max's back and up onto the monster's left shoulder. Max scooped up Barry and planted the boy on his right shoulder.

Max said, "Then let's do it. Even going slowly, we should make it to the other side before sunset."

Paul stepped in front of his friend. "Let me lead."

"But I'm taller," said Max.

"Yeah, but if you fall in, you take them with you." He pointed to Barry and Starry. "I'll be careful and stay within arm's reach just in case, okay?"

Max nodded. Paul had made a good point. He was transporting precious cargo. "Just take your time and be sure."

Paul grinned. "I will."

Bickyl took to the air. The wind produced by his wings caused Starry to tighten his grip.

"Careful with the claws, old-timer," said Max.

Starry chose not to respond.

Bickyl flew ahead. "I'll wait for you midway. There's a large outcropping of rocks. Give a scream if you get in trouble."

Paul raised an eyebrow at the dragon's comment, but thought nothing further of it.

Slowly, step-by-step, they made their way onto the Screaming Plains.

CHAPTER EIGHTEEN
DIRT NAP

BOREDOM SET IN AFTER Paul and Max had taken over 100 steps with no difficulty. The level of the soil stayed very consistent. It also remained oddly warm.
"That's 144 steps with no trouble," said Paul.
"Only 86 for me," commented Max.
"You can afford to take larger steps, Max. Paul's doing all the hard work," said Starry.
Paul placed his hand above his eyes and peered ahead. He could see Bickyl resting on a large rock outcropping. It looked like his dragon friend was sleeping. "Halfway is only another 200 steps or so. Everyone okay?"
Max smiled. "That'd be only about 90 steps for yours truly." He patted his chest with an open palm.
Starry rolled his eyes. "We're fine."
Barry had remained largely quiet during their soil stroll. He was very intent on the dirt, examining it with unease. "Hey, it's

doing something." The boy pointed to the ground around them.

Everyone stopped to look. Holes no larger than a small coin were appearing and disappearing just as quickly.

"It looks like water boiling," said Max.

"Yeah, but the soil's not any hotter than before." Paul scratched his head.

Max began to sniff the air suspiciously. "You smell that?"

Paul tested the air himself. "Smells flowery."

Starry yawned. "I bet we're just in a pocket of gas or something. I can smell it, too."

Barry's mouth opened wide, forming a perfect O. "Aahh. It smells good." He snorted in and out.

A lazy smile inched across Max's face. "It does smell nice, like witherrope daisies." His chest rose as he took in a deep breath.

Treek spilled out of Paul's belt pouch. His chittering was frantic.

Paul smiled. "Calm down, Treek." He pulled his pet closer to the ground. "Here, smell. It's so sweet, huh?"

Treek struggled out of Paul's grasp, raced up the monster's arm and onto his owner's head. Paul fell to his knees and scooped up a large sample of the dirt. He brought it close to his nose and sniffed. "That's so smelly good."

Max also hunched over, resting his knees and forearms in the soil. He laughed, "Wonder what's causin' the tweeny-tiny holes."

Barry giggled at Max. "You're talking funny, Maxie." The boy rolled off the monster's shoulder and landed on his back in the soil. He pretended to make an angel in the soil with his arms and legs.

Starry yawned yet again. "I'm so tired."

"Me too," said Paul, his eyelids drooping.

"Me three," said Max, laughing as he yawned.

Barry had stopped swinging his arms and legs, as they had sunken deep into the ground. He rested his head into the soil, allowing it to rise up to his cheeks. Barry closed his eyes. "We should take a nap…"

Everyone lowered themselves into the soil, allowing it to sweep up and cover all but their faces.

Max began to snore. Their chests rose and fell as Treek, very much wide-awake, jumped back and forth atop his fellow travelers, attempting to wake them with his hysterical screams.

The holes that had appeared so suddenly in the soil, disappeared and the strong odor of flowers drifted away.

CHAPTER NINETEEN
KILLER WAILS

Paul was enjoying a pleasant dream with talking mice and muffins holding a birthday party for him. He had just blown out the candles and was about to cut the cake when a horrible screeching cut through the air.

The dream dissolved into nothingness as Paul sat up. His eyes wildly played across the scene before him.

Tiny, shrimp-like creatures were scurrying all over the top of the soil heading away from the screaming. Max, Starry and Barry were also sitting up with looks of surprise on their faces. The screaming that had interrupted his dream was coming from the skies overhead. They all looked to see nearly a dozen winged pale yellow creatures soaring overhead. They had wild spikes of hair spilling down from their heads and surrounding their shoulders like manes. Their jaws were inhumanly extended, revealing deep-set mouths.

No wonder their screams were so frightening, thought Paul

as he struggled to rise to his knees.

One of the creatures stopped screaming and shouted at them. "Stand up and run for the rocks! Our screams won't hold them off forever." He gestured to the rocks where Bickyl stood. The dragon was surrounded by an army of the flying screamers. Each held a long spear toward the dragon, clearly preventing him from coming to their rescue.

"It's a trap!" shouted Max, his voice barely noticeable amid the screaming.

"What? We fell asleep here?" said Paul.

Max yanked Barry out of the mud and tossed Starry on his back. "There's something in the soil. Look!" He pointed a few yards away from them. Thousands of the shrimp-like creatures that had retreated from the screaming were massing around them.

Another winged creature spoke. "The Dowri will encircle you and feed if you don't head for the rocks."

Barry sniffed the air and pointed to the soil. The tiny holes that had pocked the soil earlier were returning. "That flower smell is coming back."

Starry screamed, "That's what made us fall asleep!"

Paul looked around, frozen in his tracks. *What is going on? How have we gotten so quickly in over our heads?*

Max, seeing his friend had frozen, took matters into his own massive hands. "I don't feel like taking another nap and being on those little creepies' menu." He grabbed Paul and pulled him up against his chest. Cradling his friend in his arms and with Barry and Starry secure atop his shoulders, Max plowed through the soil.

"Hold your breath, everyone," said Starry. More holes appeared in the soil underneath them, attempting to overwhelm them with the flowery gas again.

Max took long strides, heading toward the rocks holding the imprisoned dragon.

Paul said, "Aren't we going toward more trouble?"

Starry, pinching his nose tight, said in a squeaky voice, "They're helping us." He gestured at the winged creatures. "They woke us up before we became dinner."

Paul looked behind them. The Dowri, as the screamers called them, were scrambling after them, carpeting the soil with their bodies. Paul whimpered, "It looks like a million of them."

Max gulped in a breath of air. The flowery gas was strong in the air. Max stumbled.

"Stay awake, you big blue bozo!" screamed Starry.

Max wiped his eyes and regained his stride.

Paul noticed the screamers were flying slightly ahead of them, clearing their path of the Dowri with their extreme wails.

Barry said, "We're gonna make it."

Max, his face now purple from holding his breath, accelerated his pace. With a final leap, he placed them all onto the rock outcropping.

Landing on his chest, he emptied his lungs and breathed in deeply. Barry and Starry tumbled off him as Paul struggled to squeeze out from underneath his friend.

Realizing he had landed on Paul, Max rolled away and sprang to his feet. Still gasping for air, he checked on his friend. "Paul, you okay? I didn't break anything, did I?"

Paul clutched at his ribs, patting them to check that everything was in place. "I'm okay. Just gonna be a little bruised."

Max hugged his friend, lifting him away from the rocky ground. "We did it. We got away from those things."

The Dowri encircled the rocks, but did not leave the red soil.

"You brought a child to the Screaming Plains!" A booming voice from overhead brought the monsters to attention.

The largest of the winged screamers descended, landing neatly atop a big boulder. A thick beard trailed from his jaw ending well past his waist.

Bickyl rose up behind the angry speaker. His eyes were red. He too had been a victim of the soil's sleeping gases. "I didn't know. I've never been—"

The screamer snarled, "Not you, Dragon. I'm talking to the wrinkled old monster. Starry, what on Cascade were you thinking?"

Paul and Max stared at the older monster. Max said, "You know it?"

Starry sputtered, "Um, it's been a while, but I'm afraid I do. That's King Roldo, ruler of the banshees!"

"Starry, you old fool!" King Roldo raised his left arm, holding up a gem-encrusted scepter. He addressed the airborne squad of banshees that circled around him. "Escort them to the village. Let them ride their dragon, but do not give them opportunity to escape."

Several of the grounded banshees gestured with their spears for them to mount Bickyl.

"Um, I can't carry all of you, remember?" said the dragon.

King Roldo barked an order at a large banshee hovering off to his left. The banshee flew over Max and yanked him into the air with his clawed feet.

Max squealed. "Yikes!"

King Roldo said, "That will lighten your load, Dragon. Now, fly."

Barry, Starry and Paul crawled onto Bickyl's back. Paul shot Starry a look. "You know banshees?"

"Yeah, real fun guys, aren't they?" Starry coughed nervously.

Paul muttered, "Yeah, a real scream."

Bickyl rose into the air. An escort of over a dozen banshees fell into place around him. King Roldo flew up, taking the point position.

In silence, they flew to the banshee village.

CHAPTER TWENTY
BED OF FIRE

THE BED OF RICKLE worms was normally a place where the Nightmare Squire could find comforting sleep. As much as he detested it, he found he needed to rest just as much as any other magical creature. Being the Lord of the Dream Stream did not mean he could stay awake forever. The Nightmare Squire enjoyed his job, manipulating the dreams and nightmares of mortals and immortals alike. The squire controlled the flow of ideas and notions that filled the unconscious minds of sleepers everywhere. He especially took pleasure in delivering frightening, disturbing visions. Since taking over the Dream Mesa from its former owner, he had focused on sending forth frights and fears in steadily increasing numbers.

He had little desire to be on the receiving end of a nasty dream, especially one he had no hand in creating. When the Nightmare Squire slept, the Dream Stream sent him his dreams. And the Dream Stream had been sending him particularly vicious ones of late.

The Nightmare Squire's body shuddered as he curled his legs in even tighter.

This dream was filled with a fog of dread. The squire stood in a meadow of tivi wheat. The red plants rose to thigh height and were topped with a cluster of seed pods that resembled eyeballs. The sky was overcast, and a steady stream of rain was pouring down. Despite the heavy winds that buffeted the squire, the tivi wheat did not sway. The only motion in the tivi wheat was in an area almost 10 yards in front of him. The grass was parting as if something was cutting through it at blazing speed. He could not see his attacker. Whatever approached was no taller than the wheat. Shortly, the Nightmare Squire saw the face that had intruded on his dreams for the past three months. Standing only four feet away was the small boy named Barry Busman III. The boy smiled as he held out his hands.

Barry whispered, "I'm the spark." Suddenly, the tivi wheat under the boy's hands ignited into flames.

The Nightmare Squire moved to run from the rising flames, but found his feet frozen in place. He watched in horror as the fire roared over the wheat fields, sparing nothing in its path.

****

In his bed of rickle worms, the Nightmare Squire sat up, brushing away the imaginary flames that had surrounded and engulfed him in his dream.

He stepped out of bed, ignoring the stench of the now charred rickle worms. The dreams were becoming more and more vivid. While he had not been fried this time, his bedding surely had. The fire had reached out from the Dream Stream. The Nightmare Squire frowned. Powerful magic was at work here for a dream action to actually affect something in the waking world.

He marched to his throne room. Soon, the boy who had plagued his dreams would be brought to his doorstep. Once Barry entered the Dream Mesa, he could put an end to his bad dreams once and for all.

The Nightmare Squire smiled. He had much to prepare for his visitors.

CHAPTER TWENTY-ONE
CRYING KRAKEN WOLF

THE BANSHEE VILLAGE WAS impressive. Cut into the side of a canyon, mudhouse upon mudhouse was stacked atop one another. Paul noticed very few pathways or steps leading from building to building.

He looked at Starry. "How do they move about?"

Starry pointed at a flurry of activity at the far north section of the village. Half a dozen banshees with large boxes and small furniture in tow were flying back and forth between two homes. "Wings bring more freedom. Why walk up steps or climb rickety ladders when you can take to the air?"

"How will we get around?" asked Paul.

Bickyl circled, following the king toward the largest building in the village. Barry clung tight to the dragon's neck. Paul and Starry shifted their weight.

"I'm not so sure we're welcome to move about freely. King Roldo was never exactly keen on visitors," said Starry.

Paul glanced over at the banshee carrying Max. His friend looked quite sick from his flight. As Max's banshee approached the ground, he released his cargo quite early. The monster yelped as he fell nearly fifty feet to the ground. Max landed with a dull thud.

"I hope your dragon friend can manage a better landing than that," said Starry.

"Don't worry. I may not be used to carrying more than Paul, but I can still get you down with ease," said Bickyl.

The dragon glided downward, reaching the ground with little strain on his passengers. Barry slid off the dragon's neck and was the first to rush over to Max. Starry and Paul soon followed.

They looked around to see they were in a garden courtyard. Standing nearly four stories at the center of the courtyard was the most exquisite mud building. Columns of dried mud stood on either side of what was clearly a majestic palace. Each column was covered with carvings of scenes from Cascade history. Paul could see several etchings displaying life in the First Valley and the coronation of New Asgard. Each column was crowned with a large rounded dome that was made of a transparent material. Paul noticed that more greenery was contained inside the palace. The entrance was extremely tall and framed by rows of jeweled teeth. It looked much like the screaming open mouth of a banshee.

King Roldo motioned for two guards to direct the visitors into the palace. The guards fell in behind them and delivered pressing looks.

"I guess we get an audience with the king," said Paul, stepping forward.

As they entered the castle, one guard directed Bickyl to step back. They clearly didn't want him entering the palace.

Paul took offense. "Hey, Bickyl's with us. He should be allowed to come in."

One of the guards smiled. "We mean no insult to your

friend, but we fear he is too large for the entrance. If he tried to enter, he would injure himself on the sharp jewels." He pointed to the teeth rimming the entrance.

"Oh," said Paul. "Makes sense. Sorry."

The monsters along with Barry entered the palace of the banshees without their dragon friend.

****

King Roldo stood in front of the large throne, his wings folded neatly behind him. Paul got the impression the banshee king didn't often sit in his throne. They were separated from the king by a dozen rows of steep steps, the only steps they had seen in the palace. Balconies and perches were everywhere in the throne room. The king did not speak as the room filled with members of his village. Paul watched in silence as each banshee took a place inside. While the adult banshees were rather intimidating with their immense wings and teethy jaws, Paul spied a few banshees his own age. They were plump and kinder in appearance, less hardened in attitude.

"What did we do? Why all this attention?" whispered Max, directing his questions to Starry.

The older monster muttered, "Banshees care greatly for the rights of the people. The king is king in name alone. All decisions are made by the entire village."

"What are they deciding?" asked Paul.

"What to do with us," said Starry.

"Oh," replied Paul.

King Roldo surveyed the room, making a mental count of his village. By now, the throne room had filled. Nearly a thousand of his people awaited his announcement. Still, he sensed someone was missing. His heart sank as he glanced at the balcony that held his own family. His wife, Erika, and his daughter, Skelbi, were there, but his son, Tavus, was missing.

Paul noticed King Roldo was frowning. He seemed upset by a family standing on a balcony off to the king's left. Paul looked up to see a female banshee cradling a baby banshee in her arms. The mother was giving the king a look of helplessness.

King Roldo scowled. His son was a no-show yet again. He only hoped the boy had the sense not to make one of his grand appearances during their meeting. The king took two steps toward Paul and his friends. The banshee waved a crooked finger at them.

"Explain your reasons for coming to the Screaming Plains." King Roldo's voice boomed through the room.

Paul and Max stood still, uncertain what to say or do. Starry climbed the steps until he was next to the banshee king. He puffed out his webbed fins along his cheeks and declared, "While I know banshees have never been very chummy with guests, I don't think you need to take that tone with us."

King Roldo wrinkled his nose in distaste. "How dare you talk to me that way! After we risked so many of us to save you from the Dowri? How dare you!"

"We are grateful for your rescue. We are, but we didn't know the danger of the Screaming Plains. You know monsters don't leave the academy very often. We don't know our way around Cascade unless we've been assigned to spook that area." Starry stood his ground, glaring up at the king with intensity.

The banshee kneeled, bringing himself closer to the old monster. "You have seen our hidden village. We must decide what to do with you."

"Look, it's no big secret where you live. All of Cascade knows you're a private group. What? Do you think we'll leave and come back with tour groups or something?"

King Roldo's cheeks reddened. "Starry, you speak with a loose tongue. Just because you came to visit us once many moons ago does not give you a right to speak so freely!"

"Oh, just relax, Roldo. My goodness, you're even more uptight now. I'd have thought settling down and having a family would've mellowed you a bit."

The banshee crossed his arms. He looked up at his wife. His son had still not arrived. "Yes, you would've thought."

Barry marched up the steps and sat next to Starry. The boy played with the monster's tails as he addressed the king. "Thank you for saving us, sir. We didn't mean to cause any trouble."

The banshee's face softened.

"We're on a quest!" said Barry.

"You are? And what is it you seek, young man?" asked the king.

"We're going to the Dream Mesa. The Wizard Bailey told us we'd find my brother there."

"Your brother is missing?" asked King Roldo.

Barry chewed on his lower lip. "Yes, but we're gonna find him and return to Earth."

The banshee frowned. He turned to look at Starry. "You've brought a mortal back to Cascade? What were you thinking?"

Starry smiled weakly. "It was an accident. Paul opened a gate too close to the boy, and he fell through."

"Well, send him back. He should not be here." The king's strained voice was returning.

"We can't. Things are a little complicated and mysterious right now," said Starry, thinking back to how and why the headmaster had closed off the gates to Earth.

The king stared at Starry.

The old monster said, "Look, I'm trying to help him out. The Wizard Bailey said for us to go to the Dream Mesa. You want me to argue with a wizard?"

King Roldo smiled half-heartedly. "I suppose if that old dog vouches for you, then you are doing what fate commands."

"Uh, sure," said Starry. "So, you'll let us continue our quest?"

"That is for the village to decide." The king swept his arms up and glanced at his fellow banshees.

He was about to address them when a young banshee exploded into the room, nearly knocking over the guards standing by the main hall. "The wolves are here! Hurry, everyone, the kraken wolves have arrived, and they're out for blood!"

Paul noticed the boy was spotted with what looked like blood. The crowd seemed unimpressed nor shocked by his arrival. Paul and Max sent the king a questioning look.

Paul squealed, "Kraken wolves are deadly! We better do something!"

The king shook his head. "He is not a concern, monster."

The boy banshee was cartwheeling about in the air as he related how he had wrestled with a kraken wolf and barely escaped with his life. His fellow banshees seemed disinterested.

Starry, angry at the indifference in the room, said, "Kraken wolves are not a laughing matter. Summon your guards to defend the palace!"

King Roldo placed a hand on Starry's back. "Starry, there are no kraken wolves. My son, Tavus, does this all the time. He barges into meetings, crying out some absurd danger. At first, we took what he said seriously. Now, we are numb to his mischief. Today, he screams of kraken wolves. Yesterday, he spoke of the bigfoot that attacked him. Tomorrow, he'll probably moan about vampires rising up from the ocean or some such nonsense."

Starry looked at Tavus with a critical eye. The young banshee was rolling about on the floor, laughing.

King Roldo flew over to his son and pulled him up. He shrieked at him, scolding the boy for his prank. He tossed him into the air in the direction of the rest of his family. Tavus bobbled in the air as he attempted to smooth out his flight. He landed rather awkwardly on the balcony and took his place next to his mother and sister. Both acted as if he weren't there.

King Roldo addressed the village. "We must decide what to do with our visitors. Let us vote."

A voice rose from an elderly banshee settled on a perch low to the ground. The banshee stepped off his perch and shuffled across the throne room floor to stand next to the king.

"Tryler, you wish to voice your opinion?" asked the king.

"In a way. I wish for the village to decide on these visitors, but I also demand we deal with your son, Roldo." The elder banshee was bald, except for his stringy mustache braided at the tips.

King Roldo seemed taken by surprise. "What?"

"Your son cries wolf too much. He has no sense of what true danger is. Something must be done."

King Roldo looked around at his fellow villagers. All nodded at Tryler's pleas, and the king's shoulders slumped.

"Very well. We rule on the visitors and on my son. I only ask that you cast your votes without me. I cannot vote on matters concerning Tavus. It would not be proper."

Tryler nodded. "Agreed. Take your son and the visitors to the courtyard. We will come forth with our decisions shortly."

King Roldo's family joined him as they walked alongside Paul and his group—all hung their heads low as they made their way out into the courtyard. All except Tavus, who was flying here and there, chattering about monsters too horrible to exist beyond the banshee's own imagination.

CHAPTER TWENTY-TWO
BANSHEE BANISHMENT

THE MEETING TO DECIDE their fate turned out to be long. After nearly two hours, the banshees dispersed from the palace. They flew off, returning to their homes and their day-to-day routines. Tryler and several other older banshees walked out into the courtyard to address their king and the visitors. Sadness marked each banshee's face.

Tryler spoke first. "Our decision was not an easy one, Roldo."

Roldo nodded.

Tryler continued, "The visitors will leave, returning to their quest. We did not rescue them to later harm them or hide them away."

Roldo pulled his wife closer. He wrapped his wings protectively around her. His son, Tavus, was busy tickling his sister as she attempted to take a nap on a nearby patch of moss. The young banshee's screams of protest sounded more like the honking of a duck or goose.

Tryler said, "Your son has no concept of true danger. Until he does, he will continue to put our village at risk with his false alarms. Last week, Tavus put such a fright in the Olka sisters that they will no longer help with the harvest."

Hearing his name, Tavus suspended his torture session with his sister and flittered over to his father. "Ah, they're a bunch of crybabies. Got 'em good, too. Told them the Skeleton King lived under the fields, and was growing an army of bone beasts. I had buried a wergrat skull for them to dig up and when they did, they ran off in fright." Tavus laughed. "It was hilarious!"

Tryler raged, "This is the disrespect your son shows all in the village. Everything is a joke to him!"

Roldo pulled his son closer and rested the tip of his left wing over Tavus's mouth. "Quiet. Listen to your judgment."

Tryler looked over at the visitors. Paul sat on Max's shoulders, and both monsters' eyes were wide as they listened with intent. Starry, with one ear on the conversation, was assisting Barry with his duffel bag, while Bickyl was dining on triddle melons by the garden's main fountain.

"He must be educated. He must learn what true danger is. Our visitor's quest is a perfect opportunity. The village wishes to exile your son with these monsters." Tryler's voice sounded tinged with regret at the harsh decision.

Roldo squawked, "What? You can't do that! He can't leave!"

Tavus smirked.

Tryler said, "It's only for as long as they are on their quest. Once they complete their adventure, Tavus will come home and account for himself."

Paul hopped off his friend's back. "Um, we have quite a few travelers already. Not to be disrespectful, but won't Tavus be in the way?" He had no desire to have such a disagreeable banshee join their group.

Roldo was about to speak, but was silenced by his wife.

Urika stepped forth and spoke to Paul. "I think my son needs this. He is a good boy, he is. Help him like you're helping the Earth boy. Please."

Paul sucked in his lower lip and smiled. How could he refuse a mother's request?

Surprised at his wife's support of the plan, Roldo interrupted, "Urika, is this wise? Cascade is filled with dangers. You would send away your only son?"

She replied, "Roldo, look at him. He needs this. Maybe if he goes with them, he will grow a little." Tears rolled freely down her cheeks.

Roldo stood, eying his son, who for once stood still by his side. The boy had noticed his mother's emotional outburst. He was actually paying attention to the here and now instead of planning his next prank, thought Roldo. Tavus's large brown eyes were filled with uncertainty.

"What's happening, Father?" the young banshee asked.

Roldo pulled his son close to him and lowered himself to Tavus's view. "They are going on an adventure." He pointed to Paul and Max. "The village, your mother and I feel it would be good for you to go with them."

"I don't want to leave," said Tavus.

Roldo lifted his son's chin with his index finger. Their eyes were only inches apart. "I want you to do this," said Roldo. "You must learn that these wild lies of yours are wrong."

He sniffled. "I'm sorry. I won't cry wolf anymore. Please don't send me away. Please!" Tavus began thumping his tiny fists against his father's chest.

Roldo placed his hand on Tavus's shoulder. "You must leave."

Before Tavus could fly away, Max grabbed the banshee and gently pinned his wings so they could barely flutter. "Tavus, I'm Max. Welcome to the gang! I bet you'd like to know more about our quest, right?"

Without giving the banshee a chance to protest, Max

launched into an overly descriptive summary of the events to date.

Starry snorted, "Well, I'll be. First thing that beast has done right on this whole trip."

Paul looked back at King Roldo, who huddled with his wife and daughter, his head turned downward and away from his son. He waved a webbed hand at the banshee family and walked toward his dragon friend.

Max's voice filled the garden as he continued with his colorful account of their adventure. "So, your dad and his friends rescued us from those Dowri beasts. Can you believe they had put us to sleep with their gases? I can't believe I almost slept through a meal. Ha-haaa!"

CHAPTER TWENTY-THREE
TRENCH OF TOTEMS

Several banshees had escorted them to the edge of the village. King Roldo and his family had not been with them. Tavus, with the realization of his exile sinking in, had grown very quiet and mellow. Rather than fly alongside Bickyl and scout ahead with the dragon, the banshee had elected to walk with the group. They were making their way through a rather swampy area when he was stirred into action.

He spied a large rock in the water off to his left. In the misty environment of the swamp, a thorny branch that rested on the rock gave it the appearance of a creature with menacing spikes along its back. This sparked an idea for a prank.

Tavus flew into the air. He shrieked, "Climb, everybody! I see a bog beast! Hurry!"

Paul leaped onto Max's back. Starry moved closer to Barry. Max looked about. "Where? What are you talking about?"

Tavus had landed in a sagging vorrhair tree and was

attempting to bury himself in the thick, wooly leaves. "Over there! See it resting in the water? It moved! It rose up, and I saw it's horrible bug eyes! Climb a tree, Barry!"

Max walked closer to the water where Tavus had pointed. He spied the rock with the thorny branch lying across it. "That's not a bog beast, you ninny! Just a rock with a fallen branch."

Tavus giggled. "Oh, huh. I guess my mistake." He flew back down, landing next to Starry.

Paul spoke up. "You have many friends, Tavus?"

"Um, no," said Tavus.

"Ever wonder why?" asked Paul.

"Probably jealous of my dad being king," said Tavus.

Paul rolled his eyes.

Max waved a finger at the banshee. "There are enough real dangers out here. You try that again, and we'll leave you behind."

Tavus kicked at a tree root, ignoring Max.

The adventurers traveled through the swamp with no additional problems. The shadowy figure that followed them remained undetected. Its shaggy mane was cloaked in a hood, but the bones tied to its hair clinked together like wind chimes.

They were heading in the right direction, so he would not have to call upon his helpers to herd them. He did not like to owe any more favors than necessary.

Confident they remained unaware of his presence, the god, Nanabozho, kept pace with his prey.

****

With mud soaking into their pants and shoes, Paul and his troupe reached the end of the swamp. A canyon no higher than twenty feet spread out before them. The sides of the trench were steep and worn smooth from weathering and erosion.

Max spoke. "Looks like we have to head into this canyon, unless you want to wade deeper into the swamp water to find a way around it."

Paul eyed the ground. Replacing the thick mud he had trudged through was a field of small stones of dazzling color. Barry collected a few of the colorful rocks and stored them away in his duffel bag. Paul picked up a palm-sized green rock. It was round and smooth. He looked down to see the other rocks were equally smooth. "Wow, this must've been a river at one time."

"How do you know that?" said Tavus. "You talk to stones or something?"

Paul explained, "No, all these rocks are worn smooth like they've been tumbled about in water. It looks like a riverbed."

Starry hopped down from Max's shoulders, satisfied their muddy path was behind them. "I agree with Paul. Sure sign of a waterway. I think it's dried up though."

Paul eyed the sides of the canyon. "I'm not sure I like this. None of us is tall enough to climb out of here. What if there's a flash flood?"

Max flung a handful of rocks back at the swamp water, skipping several across the murky waters. "I think we'll be okay."

Starry sniffed at the air. "Can't smell a storm lurking about. It makes sense to give it a try."

Barry and Tavus had already started jogging deeper into the trench with Starry close behind. Max was following at a slower pace, but was keeping up with them due to his large strides.

Paul lingered at the mouth of the trench. "I just have a funny feeling."

Max shouted back. "Oh, relax. It's not like we're crossing a rickety rope bridge. Now, those things are death traps. Remember in The Flying Mummy comic when he fought the Killipede on a rope bridge? Aw, he's just the coolest."

From above, Bickyl glided closer to his friend. He sent the

young monster reassuring thoughts. "Don't worry, Paul. I've scouted ahead. It doesn't look like any water lies in the trench at all. It's only about a mile long, and you'll be out of it in no time."

Paul looked up at the dragon, feeling much better his friend was watching out for their path ahead. "Thanks."

"Don't mention it," said the dragon before he flew off ahead of them. "I'll await you at the end of the trench."

Paul dug into the stones at his feet. The dirt under the stones was a fine sand and seemed dry. "Okay, but be on the lookout." Paul sprinted to catch up with his friends.

****

Nanabozho placed his clawed foot over Paul's footprint. He watched his prey running headfirst into his trap. He had received the thoughts of the dragon as well. The winged beast was correct. A flood did not lay ahead of them. Nanabozho grinned. No, their death would sneak up from behind. The god removed his foot from where Paul had stood. Water seeped from the surrounding ground and erased the footprint. He reached his arms to the sky and began reciting his glorious spell. Nanabozho would exact revenge. Perhaps this time, it will mean something. Perhaps this time, his brother will return. As he chanted, the air around the Algonquin god shimmered as water rose up from the ground in an immense funnel.

****

The ground remained dry all around them. Paul was beginning to relax. While he didn't like how windy the canyon was turning out to be, he was feeling more positive they would not be caught in a surprise deluge. Up ahead with Starry, Max and Barry started whooping and hollering. Something around the next turn had captured their attention.

Paul and Tavus raced to catch up with them.

Standing nearly as tall as the canyon were rows of totem poles. They were staggered to form a zigzag pattern through the trench. Paul examined the pole closest to him. A ghoulish bear rested at the bottom, streaked with red paint to imitate fur. A wide-mouthed face of a man with very white eyes was next. A raccoon head was mounted atop the human, followed by a skunk, a deer and an eagle at the crest. The white head of the eagle looked back at where they had begun.

Max pounded his knuckles against another pole. "Solid wood." He hugged the totem and tried to move it. It didn't budge. "Really stuck in there, too."

Tavus flew up, perching himself on the head of beaver topping the third totem. He looked ahead, to see if any totems rounded the curve of the trench. "There's more of 'em ahead."

Starry scanned the totems. "Each has a human head at different heights and all the animal heads around it look fierce."

Paul peered at another totem. The human was at the top and was a woman with brown hair. Her eyes were white and wide. "The human heads look very real."

Starry added, "I noticed that, too. The animal heads are more stylized. I wonder why that is."

At that moment, a scream ripped through the air. It was Tavus flying high above the totems. His eyes were directed to the winding canyon behind them. "Water! Flash flood!"

Max frowned. The banshee was up to his old tricks again. "Oh, be quiet, Tavus. We all know you're just crying wolf. Get down here so I can wring your scrawny neck, banshee."

Max began climbing the totem nearest Tavus. This pleased the banshee. "Get up on the totems, all of you! Hurry! It'll be here any second."

Paul was about to scold the banshee himself, when he heard the rumbling of the approaching water. The ground was shaking and protesting at the arrival of the forceful guest. Paul pushed Treek into his shirt and scaled the nearest totem, the one with the woman on the top. "It's really coming! Get up now!"

Starry and Barry scrambled up a totem diagonally ahead of Paul's. Max, who had been climbing up the totem nearest Tavus, accelerated his effort and yelled, "It sounds huge!"

Paul was at the third head on the totem, when he paused to look back. Rounding the curve of the trench was a wall of water almost as tall as the canyon. It was barreling down toward them at a frightening speed. Paul pulled himself upward, gritting his teeth.

Max, who had made it to the top of his totem, crouched down and shouted at Paul, "Get movin'! Hurry, Paul!"

Paul's webbed hand reached the shoulder of the woman's head. When he grabbed it, the mouth of the woman opened wider and a scream poured forth. Shocked, Paul lost his grip and fell away from the pole. He never hit the ground. The wave of water smacked into him with the force of a steamroller. Paul lost consciousness from the weighty blow as his small frame was pulled under and tossed about inside the roving water.

Barry and Starry, who had just reached the top of their totem, screamed as they saw Paul being washed away down the canyon.

Tavus hovered above Max, his scream drowned out by the monstrous flood.

CHAPTER TWENTY-FOUR
GILL TRIP

P~~AUL TUMBLED END TO~~ end through the strong current. His thin, transparent eyelids had closed immediately upon being submerged, allowing him to see his underwater predicament with crystal clearness. He shifted in the rolling current, narrowly avoiding a large totem pole to his left. Spiralling through the water, his outstretched right arm slammed against yet another pole. The churning waters were pushing him through the trench with great speed. Paul had to gain control of his cartwheeling mode of travel before his body smashed into the side of the trench or snapped in half against one of the very sturdy totem poles. Spreading out his fingers to reveal the webbing between, he began to slow his topsy-turvy spinning.

Paul remembered what his father had taught him about wave surfing in their many visits to Oracle Beach. He used his calf fins to steer his progress, and his forearm fins and webbing helped him to further calm and guide his path. As strong as the waters were, he had stopped tumbling out of control and was weaving in and out of the totem poles with increasing ease.

His secondary gills, located behind his ears, filtered the oxygen from the water. While his family was more comfortable breathing air, their gills allowed them to breathe underwater for long spans of time. While not as efficient as the gills of a fish, Paul's gills would do in a pinch. He was grateful now for all those bathroom dunkings Max had subjected him to. Nothing like forced practice to turn an air-breather into a reluctant water-breather.

With Treek squirming under his vest, Paul remembered his pet could not breathe underwater and knew he had to get to the surface soon.

Just as he was beginning to wonder how much farther until the end of the trench, the current dumped him into a large lake. Paul swam immediately to the surface of the lake and gulped in mouthfuls of air. Treek tumbled free, gasping in lungful after lungful of air. Paul was glad his pet had survived.

Paul's transparent eyelids retreated as he looked around. Surrounding the lake were oddly stacked piles of rocks. Primitive art and symbols decorated the rock balanced on the top of each pile. While the boulders were stacked over twenty feet tall, they were not the most impressive part of the landscape.

At the direct center of the lake stood a totem pole, a grand totem pole. As wide as three of the totem poles Paul had avoided in the trench, this pole rose forty feet into the air. Paul inspected the faces on the gigantic carving. He counted more than twenty before being distracted by the powerful figure perched at the top of the pole.

Standing with arms outstretched and chest bare was a human with scarlet skin. His white hair was dressed in braids and flowed past his waist. His chest was painted with animal symbols. His pants made of animal hide and adorned with a breechcloth were dyed in such a way as to create a horizontal pattern of stripes. His moccasins were nearly hidden by the tassels fringing the bottom of each pant leg.

"Um, hello…" said Paul meekly.

The man atop the totem pole spoke with a voice that made the air quiver. "You should have drowned. How dare you deny me my revenge!"

"Umm." Paul felt slightly overwhelmed. Being battered by the rushing water and now facing a man of questionable sanity, he was at a loss for words.

"How did you survive, miserable little gnat?" He leaped down from the totem pole and entered the water with no evidence of a splash.

"I swam." Thinking a bit about his answer, Paul added, "I can also breathe underwater. Gills, you know."

The crazed man bent closer to inspect the aquatic monster. "You're not human?" he said with a hint of disappointment.

"No, I'm a monster on a quest, sir," said Paul.

"A monster, you say?"

"Yes, sir. Who are you?" asked Paul.

The man's eyes danced with fire. "I am Nanabozho." He declared his name with an air of thick importance.

"I see," said Paul, not at all sure he did see. Paul had very little contact with his fellow magical residents of Cascade, but he had taken several classes at the Monster Academy designed to fill him in on all the mysterious creatures of the realm. His mind raced through all the different possibilities. The stranger had human features. Paul thought he could be a wizard or changeling, maybe even a warlock or an elf, but Nanabozho's demanding presence seemed to indicate one clear choice. "You seem rather upset. Are you a god?"

"Yes, I am a god, little monster." Nanabozho bent to inspect his visitor more closely. "You are the first to survive my trench. Are you a powerful shaman?"

"No, just lucky to be born with gills and a solid breaststroke." Paul looked away from the god.

Nanabozho flung his arms up in the air. "You were supposed to die, crushed by the devastating might of the waters I called forth."

Paul had never met a god before. As loud as Nanabozho was, he didn't radiate a very magical vibe. "Do you try to drown everyone who travels this way?"

"I must," continued Nanabozho. "I must have my revenge."

Paul didn't understand. He remembered reading how revenge and meddling were very common in a god's lifestyle, but he hadn't actually expected it to be true. Nanabozho had a one-track mind.

"Ah, but your friends, they will not be so lucky." Nanabozho waved a gnarled finger at Paul. "Their heads will be wonderful additions to my collection." He rubbed his hands with anticipation.

"Umm, what do you mean?" said Paul.

The god shined a cruel smile. "You may have escaped my raging waters, but your friends couldn't be so lucky. Drowned by my waters, their heads will appear on my totem poles."

"You mean everyone you drown becomes a totem pole?" asked Paul.

"Yes. Each totem pole in the trench represents a foul mortal who drowned. Their height on the totem pole announces how far the waters had carried them when they pushed out their last bit of air. I've gathered quite a collection over the years."

Paul was horrified. "How long have you been doing this?"

Nanabozho thought a moment, calculating the time in his head. "Let's see, carry the 1, uh-um. Add the 7 to the 2." He traced his numbers in the air as he did his murderous math. "Oh, a little over three hundred years. Of course, your friends are the first deaths in nearly a century. Not so many visit my land anymore."

"Might have something to do with your hospitality," said a voice from behind them.

Paul and the trickster god turned to see Max, Barry, Starry

and Tavus wading through the waters of the lake, heading in their direction.

"No! Doesn't anyone know how to properly drown anymore?" screamed the angry god.

"Oh, don't be so down on yourself. You gave it a good try. If it wasn't for these totems, we'd have been a great deal less fortunate." Max sidled up next to Paul and acknowledged the large totem with a gentle thump.

"What do you mean?" asked Nanabozho. The Indian's face wrinkled in distaste.

"We hopped to safety," said Barry as he leaped in and out of the water, encouraging a great deal of splashing.

Nanabozho ignored the boy and focused his spite at Max, the largest target in the group. "Explain."

Max hoisted Paul into the air, placing his friend on his shoulders. They high-fived each other as Max explained, "Except for Paul, we all managed to climb to the top of a pole. Once we realized the water level was continuing to rise, we had to find another way to escape."

Tavus flew closer and hovered over Barry. The banshee said, "I noticed the totems were not too far apart." He beamed with pride. "I came up with the idea to hop from pole to pole."

Nanabozho's face became even more twisted. He looked at the banshee as if he were an annoying fly drawing too close to his godly face.

"We hopped from pole to pole until we arrived here," said Max.

The god shook his head as if to clear imaginary cobwebs from his head. "Resourceful, but I'm afraid your efforts were useless."

Paul replied, "What do you mean? They're alive!"

Nanabozho's voice erupted, shaking the ground beneath their feet. "My trench was not some challenge to defeat. It was your death. I will have revenge!" He swept his arms up, curling his fingers. One minute the lake was all around them, the next it hovered a few hundred feet above their head. Ignoring gravity, the airborne lake held its shape. Paul could see a variety of fish swimming about in the water. They looked as frightened as he did.

Max said, "Hey look, flying fish!"

"It doesn't matter if you can breathe underwater or quickly scramble up wooden poles! When I drop this lake on you, you'll be crushed!" Nanabozho started to fly toward the lake.

"Why are you doing this?" screamed Paul.

Nanabozho paused. "Revenge for my brother."

"But we didn't do anything," said Barry.

The god swooped down toward the boy. "You're a mortal, are you not?"

"Yes," said Barry, inching away from the god.

"And the child of a white man no less," he accused.

"Umm," said Barry.

"Back away, bozo," growled Max.

"I am addressed as Nanabozho only. Prepare to receive the same punishment my brother faced."

"We don't even know your brother," said Paul.

Nanabozho hesitated. His eyes betrayed maddening confusion. "All of you had a hand in his fate. Your jealousy drove you to drown him. I only seek to return the favor."

Starry whispered to Paul, "I don't think he's all there in the head. He's confusing us with someone else, someone who wronged his brother."

"I'm getting that," said Paul.

"Your voices tear at me. Stop squealing and greet your fate like men," said the god.

"But I'm only a boy," said Barry, his eyes connecting with Nanabozho's eyes, which narrowed to slits.

"You are old enough to suffer the sins of your people's past."

Barry hugged himself and asked, "What happened to your brother?"

"The spirits came and dragged my brother down into the waters of the unknown. I flew at the spirits in my anger. I fought with them, never showing weakness. They grew fearful and told me the secrets of the Mide."

"What's a Mide?" asked Barry.

"A ceremony with enough power to bring my brother back from the dead." Tears formed, flowing into the wrinkles lining his eyes.

"Did it work?" asked Barry.

Nanabozho turned away from the youth. "He came back."

Paul interrupted, "Why are you seeking revenge if he came back?"

Nanabozho descended to the ground, allowing his feet to touch the empty lake bed. "He came back, but he didn't stay. He left. He became the chief of the Underworld, the watcher of the dead." He kneeled next to the boy, ignoring the moist sand and mud sinking under the weight of his knees.

Barry touched the god's shoulder.

"He left me so he could be with the dead." The god sobbed.

Barry stepped closer to the crying god. "My brother is gone, too. We are trying to find him. It feels bad when your brother is away."

Nanabozho covered his face with his left hand. "Yes," he whispered.

Paul stood eying the lake overhead and the touching scene between Barry and Nanabozho. He hardly noticed when his dragon friend, Bickyl, landed quietly behind them. Starry motioned for the dragon to hang back.

"Can you visit your brother in this Underworld place?" asked Barry. It was clear the boy had no concept of the realm of death.

Nanabozho noticed this as well, and his face loosened at the boy's innocence. "No. It is too far away."

"Could you go on a quest to see him? Take some friends with you, like I'm doing?" asked Barry.

The god gently grabbed the boy's forearms. His body was drained, defeated by time and conspiring. "Violence has been a part of my life for as long as I can remember. I've plotted the fate of others, but not of myself." The god's concentration seemed misplaced. In reaction, the lake above plunged closer. Paul darted toward Barry to pull the child away from the god. He hesitated.

Noticing the boy's protector, the god smiled weakly. "Perhaps it is time I contemplate my future and put revenge in the past." Regaining his composure, Nanabozho halted the water's descent with the wave of a hand.

Looking about his surroundings with a renewed spirit, he asked, "What is your brother's name?"

"Spencer. You don't think he went to the Underworld too, do you? Maybe that's where brothers go when they get tired of their families," Barry considered, sounding as if the air had been let out of his spirit.

Nanabozho grinned, "No, I doubt it very much." The god looked up at the floating lake overhead. A decisive mask flowed over his face. He rose up into the air.

"Wait, don't go. Please, don't drown us," implored Barry.

The flying god motioned with one hand, and Barry floated upward. Soon, Paul, Max and the others were magically lifted into the sky. Nanabozho directed their bodies to a gentle landing atop the totem pole centered in the lake. All fit with room to spare.

The Indian god kneeled and spread out his arms. He stared up at the lake. "You have reminded me there are greater desires in the world than revenge. You have reminded me of family and of the power of reunion."

Barry smiled.

"While I may never see my brother again, I should not stop you from your quest." He swept his hands suddenly downward, dashing his knuckles against the hard wood of the totem. The lake above them shimmered and disappeared into thin air, fish and all.

Hearing a loud swoosh from below, they looked over the edge to see the lake had been magically returned to its home.

Barry said, "Thank you."

Nanabozho curled his lips into a weary grin. "The waters of the lake below will never again grow clouded with my rage. Perhaps there is something other than revenge a trickster god can do for a little excitement. Thank you, little brother."

Nanabozho turned and faced them, the hardness rapidly departing his eyes. "I know a few spells that might get you to where you are going a little quicker than by foot. May I help?"

"Um, how does it work? I can't say I'm too fond of traveling through a warp," said Max.

The trickster god smiled. "Think of your destination and enjoy the ride." He weaved his thumbs through the air, tracing a path filled with glowing symbols that ignited the air around them in a green flame. A large warp opened up underneath the adventurers, swallowing them whole, even Bickyl.

Max roared, "Nooooo! My stomach—"

Nanabozho, the trickster god of the Algonquin, licked his lips. Joy was returning to his heart after a long absence, and with that joy was the urgency to commit mischief. He took to the air, not even looking back as the grand totem pole in the lake crumbled to the ground. Following suit, the totems in the trench leading to the lake also vanished, releasing their trapped spirits to be greeted by Nanabozho's brother in the Underworld.

CHAPTER TWENTY-FIVE
DELIVER INTO DARKNESS

HEADMASTER STEVENS TAPPED AT the glass protecting the Monster Handbook. He received an angry shock from the magical defenses guarding the book. Smoke curled up from his singed finger. He eyed the injury with annoyance, though he was glad to see that the magic protecting the book was still in place. The book in the display case was the last copy of the original volume. It was the only copy of the manual that remained free of his tampering. The new class copies he had delivered to the students in the fall represented a revised edition. They contained all the proper chapters on being a truly scary monster, all except the final two. The dreaded chapters, which highlighted several instances where a monster's primary job is to help his intended victim, were omitted.

Since taking over the Monster Academy, Headmaster Stevens had been slowly changing the focus of the curriculum. He was under orders to add a grimmer aspect to the education process. Any teacher who had spoken out against his changes had been visited by a dazzle beast in their dreams. The dazzle beast's ability to cloud minds and erase key memories made quick work of stifling any protests to his new school mission. He was determined to produce more terrifying monsters. The most recent graduating class had been the final class not completely filled with deceitful and foul creatures. The next batch of seniors, Headmaster Stevens smiled, would be comprised entirely of horrors without a shred of goodness. His master wanted it that way. How else was he to build a grand army?

Headmaster Stevens felt his master's presence in the back of his head, buried in his unconscious. He was being called to return. His master wanted him there to witness the arrival of his most wholesome, and therefore loathsome, former students: Max and Paul.

The headmaster dashed into his office and jumped onto his uncluttered desk. He looked up at the inky blackness that hid any hint of a physical ceiling. Tendrils of dark matter coiled downward and pulled him in. Stevens reacted not with fright, but with joy. He was returning home. He swam upward, allowing the stuff of nightmares to swallow him whole.

The office of Headmaster Stevens, its desk unadorned with papers and its bare bookcase, almost seemed to sigh relief upon the departure of its latest occupant. The office had been host to many headmasters. None dripped with the deceptiveness of Headmaster Stevens.

Outside, in the waiting room, the original Monster Handbook—the only copy untouched by lies—remained in its glass case.

CHAPTER TWENTY-SIX
A THORNY SITUATION

PAUL WAS UNCERTAIN ABOUT their next move. The dimensional warp Nanabozho had sent them through had deposited them at the base of the Dream Mesa. To be more precise, it had dropped them into a thicket of twirly thorns. Only Bickyl's tough hide had spared them the sharp sting, as the dragon landed atop the thorns and the rest of their rag-tag band settled on Bickyl's padded belly.

Max was the first to slide off. He hopped over a few stray twirly thorns that lay scattered along the perimeter of the dragon's body.

"Good thing we had Bickyl here to be our safety cushion," said Max. He picked up a small twirly thorn and examined it closely. Two sharp barbs rested in the center of a fuzzy mass of roots. A tiny propeller dangled from the bottom of the plant. Max wisely held one finger against the propeller to prevent it from spinning out of his grasp. "My uncle had a run-in with these plants. Vicious bunch of carnivores."

Paul slid down next. He patted Bickyl's left wing with concern. "Are you okay?"

Bickyl responded by projecting his answer into all their heads. "I'm just fine. Twirly thorns are nasty flora, but nothing a dragon can't handle. I'm glad I was here, otherwise you'd be—"

As he dismounted, Starry interrupted the dragon's disturbing thought. "Well now, let's not dwell on what might have been. I'm sure Barry doesn't need to hear all the grizzly details, right?" Starry put special emphasis on the boy's name.

"Yes, of course," responded Bickyl.

Tavus helped Barry to the ground. The young banshee remained uncharacteristically quiet.

Max groaned and clutched his stomach. "Gotta say, warp travel just doesn't agree with me. Anyone else feel green around the gills?"

Barry nodded and covered his mouth.

Bickyl said, "I hate to be bossy, but you might want to put some distance between yourselves and these twirly thorns."

"Why?" asked Paul, scratching at his gills.

"Didn't you just totally smoosh them?" said Max.

"For the most part, but I can feel a few of them squirming underneath. There are still enough to swarm all over you."

Paul noticed a few of the scattered twirly thorns were stirring into action. Their propellers were slowly turning over. "Umm…"

"Run! I will take to the air and decoy them away from you," said Bickyl. The dragon arched its neck toward the air, preparing to lift off.

Tavus grabbed Barry and flew toward a grove of trees off to their left beyond a field of jagged boulders. Max, seeing Starry could not navigate the rock-covered landscape, scooped up the older monster and broke into a brisk jog. Paul lingered for a moment by his dragon friend.

"Can you outfly them?" Paul bit his lip.

The dragon nodded. "Twirly thorns are fast, but I'm faster. I'll draw them away from you."

Paul looked up at the dragon. The monster's eyes were worried.

"I'll be fine. I'll be back after I'm sure they won't go after you," said the dragon. "Now, go!"

Paul raced across the rocky field. He was plunging into the safety of the grove and the shelter provided by the brumbleberry bushes when he felt the downdraft from the dragon's immense wings. Paul turned to watch the dragon rise. His leather wings seemed no worse for wear from the impact. The golden dragon disappeared into the low clouds. His pursuers, over several dozen twirly thorns, swarmed after him. The hum from their spinning propellers sounded filled with anger.

Max slapped Paul on the back. "Gotta hand it to Bickyl. He's got style! A first-rate friend."

Paul smiled weakly. "He's good."

Barry was the first to ask. "What do we do until he gets back?"

The monsters looked around them, inspecting their hiding place. To their right and behind them, the grove grew thick with vegetation. Max kicked at a gnarled root that jutted out of the ground.

Starry pointed to their left. The grove thinned out, revealing another field of stones. Beyond the stones, steep walls rose upward. "The Dream Mesa is only about fifty yards that way."

"Should we try finding the entrance?" Max was already heading toward the mesa, pushing low branches away from him.

Paul said, "No, we should wait for Bickyl."

Max froze in mid-step. "Oh c'mon, we can at least head over there and find a way in. What's the harm?"

Paul said, "I'd feel better if Bickyl came with us."

Max began, "But it's not that far—"

Starry interrupted the larger monster. "I think that decision is out of our hands." He pointed with his star-tipped tails at the creatures approaching them from the direction of the mesa.

Paul's jaw dropped as his eyebrows fought an uphill battle with his forehead. Rushing toward them was an army of gruesome monsters decked out in armor of jagged bone and spikes. They looked very irritated at Paul and his friends.

Tavus moaned, "I've had enough danger to last me forever!"

Paul stood his ground and fought the urge to knock his shaky knees together. The largest of the monsters, a green-skinned lizard with clusters of tentacles surrounding his rows of teeth and two arms sprouting from either side of his torso, brought the army to a stop and pointed his oversized spear at Paul's chest.

Treek coiled around his young owner's neck and hissed at the threat.

Paul's brow furrowed with dread. *What have we gotten into?*

CHAPTER TWENTY-SEVEN
TERROR TROOP TUSSLE

THE LEADER SPOKE WITH a chorus of hisses trailing each sentence. "The Nightmare Squire wants these puny monsterssssss? They look sssso pathetic and weak!"

Paul detected frustration in the monster's voice.

"His judgment must be at a lossssss," said the lizard monster.

A wider monster covered in a tortoise-like shell marched up alongside the outspoken commander. His voice sounded slow, but forceful. "Watch your words. Our master doesn't take kindly to criticism. You of all creatures should know that." He nodded toward the lizard's lower left arm.

Paul glanced down and noticed the lizard held the spear with only three strong arms. The fourth arm was little more than a stump. A black cloud of energy floated where the arm ended at the elbow. It was obvious the lost limb still caused its owner pain from the way the lizard favored his right side.

Tavus squawked at the sight of the missing lower arm and took flight. He zoomed away, screaming his banshee wail in all directions.

Several of the monsters moved past Paul, heading after the banshee. The lizard blocked their pursuit with his spear. "Leave the little pesssst. His screams are of no importance. The Nightmare Squire only wants the boy and his monstersssss."

The soldiers nodded, their eyes betraying disappointment at not being able to give chase.

"Something isn't right here," offered Starry.

Paul confronted the nearest soldier. "What are you?"

The shelled creature puffed out its chest and proclaimed, "We're the elite army of the Nightmare Squire. We are his Terror Troops! I am Zargal, Lieutenant-at-Arms." He gestured to the foul-tempered lizard. "Our commander is General Shatter! We—"

The lizard snarled at his second-in-command, "They don't need to know our namesssss! Sneak back into your shell, fool!"

Zargal snaked his long neck back into his shell so that only his snout stuck out.

The lizard remarked, "Bah, enough with thisssss. I was only asked to deliver them to the master. What he does with them is his businessssss." The lizard paused, allowing his long yellow tongue to journey across his teeth. "You ask me, it's hard to believe he wants us to treat these weaklings as guestssssss."

Resting on Max's shoulder, Starry whispered, "This is definitely not sounding good. You should do something."

"Like what? All of those guys are bigger than me. Even that flying starfish thing." Max pointed to a shifty-eyed monster that hovered above them like the roof of a circus tent. Its five bulbous eyes arranged above its sharp beak at the center opened and closed without making a sound.

"Barry's safety matters most. We must get him away." Starry's eyes pleaded. "Cause a ruckus, stir up some trouble, and I'll get Barry away. You're good at aggravating others. Put that talent to use, for Pete's sake!"

Max frowned. "You're a nasty old monster." He moved to kneel, extending his right arm so Starry could easily dismount. "You're a troublemaker, which explains how I can both love you and hate you."

Starry smiled. He looked over to the commander of the Terror Troops who paid him little notice. General Shatter was still scolding Paul and his own men.

Max chuckled as he looked around for a suitable distraction. His eyes fell on the drooping arms of the starfish above them. He smiled slowly. Grabbing the nearest arm, Max began to spin the floating umbrella about. It squealed in surprise at being twirled. Other members of the Terror Troops took notice and rushed Max with their sharp weapons at the ready.

Max whipped the starfish around one last time before releasing it toward the approaching troops. The creature instinctively spread out its five-pronged body and smashed into his fellow soldiers.

Max looked around to see Starry and Barry had escaped. He was greeted, however, with the weighted end of Commander Shatter's second weapon, a spiked mace.

Max's last sight as he fell unconscious was of Starry and Barry being lassoed by a many-horned bruiser and dragged back into captivity. His distraction had been for nothing. They were all captives of the Nightmare Squire—all except for a spineless banshee.

CHAPTER TWENTY-EIGHT
TALL DRINK OF WATER

THE DREAM MESA WAS an impressive outcropping, rising up nearly a mile before disappearing into dark clouds. Its sides were sheer rock with very few grooves or crevices available for climbing. Paul estimated its diameter at nearly 500 feet. Large and small boulders were stacked in teeter-totter fashion around the base. Paul saw no entrance, although that didn't stop his captors. The Terror Troops marched up to the base of the mesa and stepped right through the solid rock. Paul's eyes widened as he watched each monster before him step into the stone. The rocky surface that swallowed up each soldier shimmered unnaturally. Soon, the only ones left to enter the Dream Mesa were Paul, his friends and Commander Shatter. Ahead, Max was putting up quite a fuss.

"Look, if you think I'm stepping through there, you've got another thing coming." Max was backpedaling away from the rock. The lizard was pushing him forward with his three good arms.

"Just enter, fool. It's a hidden entrance, masked by an illusion spell. It won't harm you, but I surely will if you put up any more of a fight." Shatter's eyes narrowed to tiny slits.

"Go ahead, Max. It'll be okay," urged Paul. He didn't have the heart to admit his own stomach churned with uncertainty. He felt very threatened by where their adventure was leading them, but also felt equally out of control to stop it.

Max disappeared into the stone. A brief moment later, his head reappeared. He smiled weakly, "It's okay in here. Not exactly cheery in the decor department, but we're not walking into a fiery pit of lava or anything."

Paul and those remaining entered the Dream Mesa.

Once inside, Paul was distressed to see how dull and uninspiring the interior truly was. They made their way through a maze of branching caves, all cut into the rock with an eye for consistency and minimal roughness. About every eight feet, a will-o-wisp lantern hung on black hooks mounted into the curved walls.

They proceeded in silence. Paul lost count of the many twists and turns they took. He tried to remember which tunnels they selected when they came upon a choice of routes, but soon gave up. The only thing he knew for certain was that they were heading slowly uphill, rising higher and higher. He also noticed that their large escort dwindled as they moved on. Soldiers in their party left the group in pairs or trios until there was only the commander and his second-in-command, Zargal. The tortoise creature led the way with a great deal of enthusiasm.

They were entering a tunnel that was twice as wide as the rest and was decorated with glowing paintings of primitive symbols of power and magic. The walls seemed to hum with hidden power. Gesturing with his stubby claws, Zargal spoke in the informed tone of a tour guide delivering an assigned speech. "We're entering the heart of the mesa. Soon, we will be in the core where the Dream Stream flows. The images etched on the walls signify dreams of power and strength. My father helped weave these paintings into the rocky walls. He was a powerful wizard who served faithfully."

Barry whispered to Starry, "This is like our field trip to the planetarium. There's a hall you walk through where all the constellations are glowing purple on the wall. The light makes the white clothing glow. I always loved to wear my white sneakers on that trip."

Starry nodded. The monster was relieved the boy could not sense the tension and dread that weighed on the rest of them.

The tunnel opened up onto a narrow ledge that looked out over an immense cavern. Paul could see that the ceiling of the cavern was almost 100 feet above their heads, while the floor of the cavern was double that distance. No will-o-wisp lanterns shed light on their arrival. Instead, the radiant glow from a stream of bright blue water that defied gravity and flowed vertically up through the center of the cavern gave them ample light.

Zargal announced, "Here we stand before the Dream Stream!"

Paul was overwhelmed by the sight. The stream flowed out of an impressive hole below and disappeared at the top in a hole equally as large. He had no idea magic existed that could create such a unique stream. "How does it do that? Where does it go?"

"The Dream Stream is ancient magic, older than legend. It pours forth from the heart of the earth and flows into the endless sky above."

"You mean it pours into the sky?" asked Starry.

"In a manner of speaking," said Zargal.

"You mean, if we went to the top of the mesa, we'd see the Dream Stream flowing deep into the sky?" asked Max.

Barry was captivated by the rolling waters. "You can see things in the water."

The tortoise nodded. "Those are dream images flowing by. Everything ever dreamed travels through the Dream Stream."

Paul noticed the bright blue of the stream did not extend throughout the column of water. Over half of the liquid was as black as charcoal. "Why's it so dark down there and so blue in the upper part?"

"That would be the work of our newest master. The Night—" Zargal was knocked to the floor, struck from behind.

All turned to see what had hit their guide, expecting to see Commander Shatter's toothy grin. Instead, a tiny gremlin no more than a foot or two in height flitted through the air.

"Loose lips sink ships, Zargal. Your father had the same character flaw. Pity such weakness runs in the family." The gremlin kicked at the hard shell of the monster under his feet.

Zargal grunted, but did not reply.

Paul said, "Hey, why'd you do that?"

The gremlin snorted and scratched around in his large ears with his forefingers. "Because, anything worth learning about properly should be presented from the authority, the person in charge."

Barry asked, "Are you the Nightmare Squire?"

Paul and Max shook their heads. The tiny beast was not the creature from their disturbing dreams.

"No, he's a mere underling. Swinky, please introduce me properly to our guests. And none of your nicknames for me either." The voice rumbled forth from the Dream Stream. It was thick and raspy.

"Oh, yes, of course." Swinky flew over to the edge of the water, dipping his tiny claws into the crystal blue waters. Where he had touched the stream, it flowed inky black. "I present to you…the Nightmare Squire!"

A black scab of water appeared on the Dream Stream. Walking out from the stream was the figure from Paul's and Max's dreams.

"Here's where things get nasty," said Max.

Paul gnawed at his bottom lip, nodding solemnly at his friend's comment.

CHAPTER TWENTY-NINE
BOND OF BROTHERS

JUST LIKE IN THEIR dreams, the Nightmare Squire was shrouded in darkness. His hair billowed in the air, seeming alive and ready to snake out and grab anything that dared to stray too close. It was his teeth that again rattled both monsters. Paul couldn't take his eyes off the white fangs, as the ruler of the Dream Mesa addressed them.

"Welcome to my home. I am so pleased to see all of you," said the Nightmare Squire.

"Um, you were expecting us?" asked Barry.

The Nightmare Squire kneeled and placed a bony hand on the boy's shoulder. "Of course, I was. I'm here to help." He stood up and looked at the new arrivals. "I can help all of you."

Starry glared at the ruler of the Dream Stream. "You're new to the Dream Stream, aren't you?"

The Nightmare Squire replied, "Yes. I've been at this dream business for only about a year. It's a great deal of work, but quite rewarding."

"What do you do?" asked Barry.

"I manage the Dream Stream, making sure it continues to flow. I create dreams and nightmares and drop them in the stream. They make their way into all the sleeping minds of the world."

Barry said, "But why send out nightmares?"

The squire hesitated, then answered. "Well, dreams and nightmares help sort out real problems in the waking world. They also keep your brains busy while you sleep. Minds are always hungry for stimulation, and I'm their nighttime source. I offer inspiration and desperation to all."

"But I don't like nightmares." Barry stuck out his bottom lip.

"Well, then I've done my job, Barry," said the Nightmare Squire. "Nightmares help deliver warnings. They stir people to action. Part of the reason you are here is the recent nightmares you've received, right?" He shot a knowing look at Paul and Max.

Both monsters nodded, slightly ashamed.

"Why don't you call yourself the Dream King?" asked Barry.

The squire smiled. "My, you certainly are a fountain of questions, aren't you?" He snapped his fingers, and Swinky dove into the Dream Stream only to return a moment later with armloads of folding chairs in tow. The chairs glowed a dark purple and dripped stardust as he opened them up and invited their guests to sit.

Paul asked, "Um, are they real?"

Swinky huffed, "Of course, they are. At least, they exist as long as you keep them in the Dream Mesa. Anything made of dream stuff disappears into thin air if it leaves the Dream Mesa and is not involved in a dream or nightmare."

Paul, Max and Barry sat down. Only Starry remained standing.

"To answer your question, Barry, I could call myself the

Dream King, but my specialty is crafting nightmares," the Nightmare Squire declared. "Not to say I don't create dreams. I wouldn't be doing my job properly if I didn't spread fanciful thoughts, after all."

Max said, "Well, that's all well and good, but why are we here? The Wizard Bailey wasn't too clear about that. He just said to come to the Dream Mesa."

"Wizards. They're even harder to understand than the most puzzling dreams," said the Nightmare Squire.

Starry noticed the squire quivered slightly at the mention of the powerful wizard.

The Nightmare Squire continued, "You are on a quest, all of you. You are also searching for Barry's brother, Spencer. What you don't know is the two of you are searching for your place in the world. Let's face it, you've pretty much messed up any chance of a decent spook career through the typical jobs monsters take upon graduating, right?"

Paul and Max nodded.

"Well, all your answers rest within the Dream Stream." The Nightmare Squire held open his arms and gestured grandly toward the magical waterway.

He yanked Paul out of his chair and slung an arm around the monster's shoulder with affection. "I have need of scary monsters such as yourself, Paul. My Terror Troops, whom you've met, are my army of spooks. They travel through the Dream Stream delivering fits of fear to those who sleep. Now, doesn't that sound so much more fulfilling than haunting a simple pillow or sock drawer?"

Paul said, "Um, sure." The Nightmare Squire's voice made the hairs on the back of his neck rise.

"And you, Barry," proclaimed the ruler of the Dream Stream. "I have the answer to your quest." He floated over to the Dream Stream and touched its edge with the tip of his forefinger. Sparks spilled forth, and the color of the water grew inky black. An image began to form in the dark waters.

Barry climbed down from his chair and walked to the edge of the cliff for a closer look. He squinted and asked, "What is it?"

The scene in the water became clearer. A mob of hideous beasts of every horrible shape and size imaginable were attacking a lone figure atop a rocky outcropping. Barry zeroed in on the figure. He recognized the short spiked hair and wide eyes of his brother. "Spence!" he cried.

"Your brother is trapped!" said the Nightmare Squire.

"Then get him out, you fool," said Starry. He rose up on his hind legs and growled.

The Nightmare Squire shrugged his shoulders and held out his open hands in a gesture of helplessness. "I wish I could, but I can't."

"Well, if he's trapped in the Dream Stream, you should be able to get him out. Heck, for all we know, you put the poor boy there in the first place," snarled Starry, growing more and more upset.

"He is not in the Dream Stream. If he were, I could retrieve him quite easily. He is in another dimension, trapped by magical spells beyond my understanding. I can use the Dream Stream as a window to other worlds, but I assure you Spencer is trapped nowhere in my realm." The Nightmare Squire's eyes flashed with power.

"We have to get him!" said Barry.

"The spells prevent me from entering, but the barrier can be penetrated by a blood relative of the boy's. Barry can break the spell and you can pass through to help the child," said the Nightmare Squire.

Barry turned and pleaded to his monster friends, "Please, we have to go! Please!"

Deep in the pit of Starry's stomach, a sense of unease uncoiled like a snake.

CHAPTER THIRTY
THE GRAVITY OF THE SITUATION

THE BANSHEE HAD WATCHED them disappear into the side of the mesa. One minute, they were there; the next, the rock had swallowed them up. Tavus had flown away in fright. Upon realizing no one was in pursuit, he had carefully doubled back to watch his friends enter the Dream Mesa.

Tavus felt very alone. Back home, among the hustle and bustle of his village, there was always someone around. Here, perched on a branch, hidden by thick clumps of leaves and vines, a shiver ran up his spine. No one was here. He couldn't scream out his fears. He couldn't shout for a mighty rescuer.

He had no idea if Bickyl would be back and was fearful he might be caught by one of the horrible creatures who had taken his friends. Every muscle in his body prompted him to fly away, to run from danger, but Tavus surprised himself. He swooped down from his hiding place and flew straight toward the rocky mesa wall. He landed a few feet from the Dream

Mesa and extended a hand to test the stone. His fingers disappeared into the rock. Filled with anxiety, he stepped through the rock. He waded through the dark for almost ten seconds before his eyes began to adjust to the dim light inside.

As his surroundings became clearer and brighter under the will-o-wisp lanterns, Tavus saw he had stepped into a long tunnel that extended in either direction.

Which way did they take his friends? How many of those horrible monsters were there?

The tunnel was not wide enough for him to risk taking to the air and his father had warned him not to fly in tight places. Instead, he quietly shuffled down the tunnel to his left, heading deeper and downward into the Dream Mesa.

At the first branching, he chose the passage to the left. Roaring and snorting was coming from the right, and Tavus had no desire to stumble across any horrible beasts. The tunnel the banshee chose was filled with tiny clumps of purple mushrooms rimming the edges of the floor. He was careful to avoid them, uncertain if they posed a threat.

After trekking through the tunnel for over five minutes, he heard the echoes of voices coming from ahead. Their conversation was filled with angry grunts and crude barks. He slowed his pace and strained his ears to determine if the voices were growing louder or fainter. After listening for over a minute, he decided the voices were fading and the owners of the horrible noises were walking away from him. Tavus waited for silence to return to his tunnel before proceeding.

Finally satisfied the voices were long gone, he moved forward again. Around the next bend, he encountered another intersection. Four different paths presented him a wealth of choices, though each looked the same. He headed left again, thinking it might be wise to stay consistent with his direction choices in case he needed to backtrack. Truthfully, Tavus was uncertain he could find his entry point into the mesa, but he wanted to feel like he had some sense of his route through this twisting underworld. He continued on, noticing the sharp downward slope of the tunnel he had selected. The tunnel wound left and right, meandering back and forth like an aimless river. The path grew steeper, and Tavus thought it odd the builders of the tunnel had not carved steps. Using the wall, he steadied himself as best he could. He considered turning around and trying another tunnel. If the tunnel grew any steeper, he would be in serious danger of sliding downward out of control.

He was just about to turn around and climb out of the ill-chosen tunnel when he heard voices from behind. They were growing louder quickly. Someone was coming toward him. Tavus sped up. For better or worse, he would have to brave the steep slope. His hands scrambled across the rocky wall to steady his progress. He was thankful for his sharp claws. Once, when his feet slipped and he started to tumble down, his claws dug into the hard rock and gave him time to regain his footing. As quickly as he tried to move, however, the travelers behind him seemed to be going even faster. Their voices continued to grow louder. Tavus could make out snippets of the conversation.

One voice sounded like gravel. "…Squire sure can spin a lie."

Another was high-pitched and metallic. "He even had me believing his story. Those suckers don't know what they're in for."

Tavus tested his wings, thinking maybe he could fly down through the tunnel. He fluttered them briefly. The tunnel was wide enough, but it twisted around so much that he wouldn't be able to avoid scraping against the walls and damaging his wings. He would have to continue on foot. Tavus risked a look back and saw the long shadows of the unknown strangers on the rock walls. There were three of them and, they weren't small.

He stubbed his foot on a loose stone, causing it to bounce

down the path. The noisy rock produced echoes throughout the tunnel.

Everything grew quiet behind the banshee. The shadows on the wall froze. Tavus also froze, halting his breath as he listened for the creatures' next move. He detected whispering, but could not make out the words.

He hoped they would run for help and give him enough time to find a decent hiding place. The banshee was not so lucky. The shadows behind him began to move forward again.

Tavus bolted down the tunnel, carelessly ignoring the steep winding slope. He lost his footing on a clump of mushrooms and fell forward. He slid downward, captive to gravity and the world's rockiest curly slide. His wings bashed against the wall as he spiraled.

Tavus screamed as he plummeted deeper into the Dream Mesa.

CHAPTER THIRTY-ONE
GOING WITH THE FLOW

HE MADE IT SOUND so simple. Jump into the Dream Stream, enter the other dimension, frighten off the beasts attacking Spencer and bring the boy back to safety. Starry knew it was more complicated than that. The Nightmare Squire was holding something back.

"You'll be reunited with your brother in no time," said the Nightmare Squire.

Barry smiled. He adjusted the straps on his backpack, tightening them for a snug fit.

"What's stopping those creatures from tearing the boy to shreds?" asked Starry.

"I truthfully don't know. Some sort of force field or spell, perhaps," said the Nightmare Squire. "All I know is what the Dream Stream tells me."

"The water talks to you?" asked Paul.

"Yes. It speaks to me within my own dreams and

nightmares. It urged me to seek out Barry."

"Did it tell you Barry could rescue his brother safely?" asked Starry. The older monster was determined to shake the truth from the Nightmare Squire.

Swinky said, "Look, buddy, my boss is telling you like it is. Drop it down a notch."

Starry stared at the hyperactive gremlin. "Barry is my responsibility."

"Starry, he's our responsibility," said Paul. "We're here to help him." Paul sounded uncertain.

Starry smiled. The young monster was coming around. He was starting to realize there was more to life than well-placed bumps in the night. "I just don't..."

"We gotta try," said Paul.

The Nightmare Squire thumped Paul and Max on the backs. "You boys go rescue that boy, and then we'll settle down to talk about your future."

The young monsters looked at Starry. The older monster nodded. "Go with Barry and bring them both back safe and sound."

"What about you?" asked the Nightmare Squire.

"I'm staying put. I wanna keep my eye on you to make sure nothing fishy is going on. I don't like being double-crossed."

The Nightmare Squire raised his left hand as if preparing to recite a pledge. "Wouldn't dream of it."

Barry asked, "So, how do we get in there to Spencer?"

"Grab hands and leap into the Dream Stream. It will take you to your destination." The Nightmare Squire bowed.

Barry jutted out his hands. Paul and Max clasped hold of them tightly. The little boy looked at the monsters and said, "Here we go!"

Barry Busman with Paul and Max in tow, leaped into the Dream Stream. They were instantly swallowed up in the current.

Starry watched as the threesome floated up the waterway,

looking for any signs of distress on their faces.

He lost sight of them when they hit a black patch of the stream and dissolved into darkness.

The Nightmare Squire turned to the older monster and said, "Well, that's that. All that's left to do now is await their return. Care for a nibble of dinner?" he asked.

Starry shook his head and stared at the steady current of the Dream Stream.

CHAPTER THIRTY-TWO
WORM FOOD

TAVUS NEARLY LOST HIS head on the final bounce of his fall. He ducked barely in time to avoid crashing into a large stone pillar that came out of nowhere. He rolled to a stop in an immense cavern. The pillar behind him was impressive. Carvings of all manner of ghastly creatures twisted in and around each other as if engaging in some bizarre stone dance. To either side of the pillar were rows of other pillars. Each depicted scenes of horribly misshapen monsters cut into black stone.

Of course, the pillars were overshadowed by what arose from the center of the cavern. Spilling forth from the ground was a stream that flowed up into the air and disappeared into a ceiling over 300 feet above. Tavus had never seen water run uphill. Even more impossible, this water ran up through thin air. He rubbed his eyes, thinking they were playing tricks on him. He looked at the center again. The water continued to flow skyward. His village would never believe such a thing. The young banshee was not naïve. He knew magic filled the world of Cascade, but this waterway was so much more. It seemed to be winking at the impossibility of its own existence.

The banshee's thoughts were cut short by the arrival of his pursuers. Three wormlike monsters snaked their way easily out of the steep tunnel he had just descended. Spikes and clumps of armor speckled their bodies as they slithered toward Tavus.

The worm with the largest mandibles screamed at him, "There's the little noisemaker! Recognize him, Louzol?"

The smallest of the worms replied, "No, Earyib. Might be that outsider Shatter mentioned. Should we eat him?"

The third worm merely licked his mandibles with anticipation at the idea.

Earyib said, "Nah, looks stringy. Let's capture him and take him up to the boss. I smell a promotion."

"Ah, Earyib, you always think two steps ahead," said Louzol.

"That's what separates me from you and Dulpie—ambition!" said Earyib as he slithered closer to Tavus.

The banshee stepped back, inching away from the pillars and toward the stream. He saw a tunnel on the far end of the cavern, much too far for him to run. Or maybe not.

The lead worm saw him eyeing the tunnel. "Awful long way to run, little monster. Think I'm slow, do you?" The worm sped up.

Tavus turned and ran. The worm screamed at him. Tavus felt the worm was almost on top of him. He would never make it to the tunnel. Then, he was struck with the most obvious plan. He stretched out his wings in the large cavern and flew toward the ceiling.

Below him, Earyib lunged upward in an attempt to snatch at his now airborne prey. He missed the banshee with his clacking mandibles, but did hit the young monster with a bone spike. Tavus, knocked off course, plummeted into the waters of the

Dream Stream. His wailing was soon lost in the decisive flow of the waterway.

Earyib dropped to the earth. Louzol teased his friend, "Guess you're not as good at moving up as you thought."

Earyib flexed his midsection, tossing a wave of stones at the annoying worm.

Louzol said, "Should we tell the boss?"

Earyib replied, "Nope. He'd fry us for letting the runt escape. Let's just keep it our little secret."

Louzol nodded. "Okey-dokey. Let's go get some grub."

The three worms raced back up the tunnel with thoughts of food on their minds.

From behind the tallest pillar, Swinky flew forth. He shook his head at the retreating worms. "Grand Master Dreamy Dream is gonna be very distressed. I told him he can't trust those horrid worms. Bunch of low-lifes, every one of them."

Swinky twirled and floated toward the Dream Stream. The banshee might stumble across the true plans of his master. He rolled up imaginary sleeves and plunged into the stream. "Time to put an end to our little banshee problem before he screams out the truth. Not that anyone would believe him." Swinky laughed.

Having viewed the dreams of the world's creatures, Swinky was aware of many personal weaknesses. He knew just the thing for taking care of a banshee who cries wolf.

The gremlin navigated through the currents of imagination with ease. In his wake, the waters of the stream became clouded with blackness.

CHAPTER THIRTY-THREE
SWIMMING UPSTREAM

BARRY WAS SURPRISED HE could breathe inside the Dream Stream. The water tasted a little gritty and salty, but it entered his mouth and filled his lungs with oxygen.

As instructed, Barry held tight to his friend's hands. All around them, strange oddities floated by to fulfill their roles inside the dreams or nightmares of creatures everywhere. Rolling through the waters to the left was a lighthouse with hundreds of glowing eyes mounted where the light should be. A herd of what could best be described as shrimp ponies galloped by on the right. Atop each pony was a small block figure dressed in black and holding a frying pan in its clawed hands. Barry whispered a thank you that his own imagination had never visited him with such frightening dreams.

They traveled through the Dream Stream taking in the sights. A bearded caterpillar astride a rocking chair, five dwarves dressed in bubble gum, a pair of playing cards wearing nightcaps, and even wilder images flowed by them. Apparently content with their destinations, none of them fought the current.

Upon reaching their intended exits from the waterway, each bizarre image bobbed gently into snake-like tubes that ran off in all directions from the Dream Stream.

Paul thought, *I didn't see any tubes on the outside. That's odd.*

Probably because they are invisible outside of the Dream Stream. Max's thoughts clattered into Paul's and Barry's minds.

Hey, I can hear you like Bickyl. You're both talking in my brain, thought Barry.

Wow, thought Paul.

How do we know where to find the exit to that dimension holding Spencer? thought Max.

The Nightmare Squire told us to think of my brother and we would be brought to where he is, thought Barry. The boy closed his eyes and concentrated on his brother. His monster companions followed his example.

One minute, they were flowing through the Dream Stream; the next, they were lifted out of it and tumbling through an exit hose. The hose dropped them onto a sandy plateau. Deformed cactus spotted the landscape in purples and greens.

Max hopped to his feet. "Good thing we didn't land on one of those. Thorns like that are not what I want to snuggle up against."

Paul brushed the sand from his legs. Barry had scampered to the edge of the plateau and was looking down with rapt attention.

"Careful, Barry! We have no idea how far up we are," cautioned Paul. He grabbed the boy's upper arm as he also peered over the edge.

The ground lay over twenty feet below, and there was Spencer, surrounded by a dozen nasty creatures.

"Man, are those guys ugly!" said Max, whistling

affectionately to punctuate his statement.

"Spencer! Up here!" yelled Barry. "We're here to rescue you!"

Spencer looked up and smiled. His lips spread wide to reveal endless rows of black teeth.

Barry fell backward. His eyes wide. "B-b-blub!"

Paul thought aloud, "What's going on?"

Spencer—or the creature that was pretending to be Spencer—answered, "Why simple, little monster. It's dinner time!"

"Oh, crud, those things can climb," said Max.

Below them, the creatures led by Spencer were clawing their way up the side of the plateau.

"I don't understand. The Nightmare Squire said Spencer was…" Barry was beginning to cry.

"Absolutely gullible, Paul and Max. I expect better of my students," said a voice from above. The threesome looked to the sky to see Headmaster Stevens flowing out of the dark, starless sky. "How rude. Have you no greeting for a former acquaintance?"

Headmaster Stevens smiled broadly to reveal glistening black teeth.

CHAPTER THIRTY-FOUR
TRIFLING WITH THE TRUTH

THE TIME FOR SUBTLETY was over. The blotches of cruelness the Nightmare Squire had seeded in the river were growing. The Dream Stream had to act now to reveal the truth or all would be lost. If the waters carrying all dreams fell to darkness, reality would soon follow. Because Tavus had entered the waters without being clouded by the deceit of the Nightmare Squire, the Dream Stream focused its essence and the purest of truths at the waters surrounding the banshee. The waterway sensed the young monster was in a state of panic, his thoughts jumbled and tinged with fear. He was not the ideal audience for its message, but the stream hoped the banshee would see what was happening.

****

Tavus gulped mouthfuls of water, attempting to catch his breath. Unlike that in the lake near his village, this water didn't choke him and fill his chest with fluid. Instead, he found he could breathe it easily. He swam as best he could through the waters, avoiding the odd objects and creatures that paraded around him. He saw no sign of the worms. Maybe he had outrun them. Of course, the other possibility also raced through his mind: they were afraid to enter the river for some reason. *Is there something worse in these waters?*

None of the unusual things he had seen pass by, had attacked him. The spider with telescope eyes, the snoring mailbox and the firecrackers that smelled of lemons had all floated past without incident. In fact, the girl whose head had orbiting rings had even smiled at him. And the flock of gold coat hangers had hummed a friendly tune in his direction.

He was beginning to get the hang of navigating through the water. He avoided the dark patches of water. They radiated an evilness that made the banshee queasy. The pure blue waters of the magical river, however, filled Tavus with positive sensations. He felt invited and welcome. Despite those feelings, he desperately wanted to find a way out of the vertical waterway. He tried swimming in every direction, except against the current. No matter how far he traveled, he never broke the surface of the river. Recalling the river was not that wide in the cavern, Tavus concluded the river was magical and slowed his paddling, allowing the strong current to push him forward and upward.

Would the river end among the clouds or stretch farther with stars all around? He had flown up to touch the clouds, but had never even attempted to venture high enough to reach the stars. His father had claimed it impossible, the air being too thin among the stars. Tavus was not eager to test his father's theory and hoped the waters would flush him out soon, so he could regain some control over his journey.

He was anxiously thinking what to do, when the river

thankfully revealed his next course of action. He knew once he saw it that it was the true path and not a cruel trick or trap. Deep inside, his spirit hummed in agreement with this sign, and a sign it truly was. Mounted atop a large wooden doorframe that rested on a bundle of dirt and rocks was an enormous yellow sign that read: TAVUS! Enter here to receive the truth!

The banshee didn't know how, but he sensed the river was communicating with him. He paddled to the door and grabbed the simple brass knob to heave it open. It swung freely, not even registering the massive weight of the water around it. He dove through the doorframe.

****

The gremlin was closing in on his prey. Stopping to dart in and out of the dark patches of the river to recharge his energy had slowed him down a bit, but the patches were more plentiful than in other trips he had made into the Dream Stream. He had his master to thank for that. Soon, the waterway would be completely dark, and he would move more freely. He had just exited a dark patch to see the banshee floating into a doorway. He cursed and shoved himself forward. The door was closing slowly behind the banshee. Swinky had to get through before it shut or he would never catch up to him. What was the Dream Stream up to? As the door inched closed, it began to dissolve into dream stuff. Swinky didn't have much time.

The gremlin propelled himself madly forward and slipped through the narrow opening. His tail slithered through, nearly caught by the door clicking shut. The dream door faded into nothingness as it rejoined the magic in the waters of the Dream Stream.

****

Tavus was surprised water no longer surrounded him. Upon entering the door, he had been transported to the top of a large rock. The rock jutted out from a bank of clouds. He was very high. Above him, stars twinkled their greetings, almost close enough to touch.

Tavus had no trouble breathing. The air was not thin at all. *So much for his father's theory,* he thought. Then again, he was overcome by the feeling that he was not in the real world. Everything around him looked clear when he focused on it, but he noticed that his surroundings grew fuzzy if he didn't maintain his concentration. It reminded him of a dream.

"This is a dream, little banshee. Trust your thoughts." The voice rumbled forth all around him. He couldn't pinpoint who or what was talking. "Who said that?"

"I don't have much time. I need you to deliver the truth. Can you do that?" pleaded the voice.

The banshee noticed that the stars dimmed when the voice spoke and the rock under his feet seemed to vibrate. It was as if his surroundings were speaking to him. "Um, I'm not exactly someone people are quick to believe anymore."

"Your friends need you, Tavus. I need you to share the truth, or else evil will pollute my waters." The voice sounded urgent.

"Your waters? I don't understand." The banshee shivered in the cold air atop the rock.

"You are still in the Dream Stream. I just gathered up dream images to make this place so you would be more comfortable."

"Who are you? What's going on?" said Tavus.

"See the truth," the voice whispered.

The air in front of the banshee shimmered. A picture formed. It showed a boy sleeping soundly in a bed. The banshee stepped closer.

The boy looked much like an older version of Barry. "That's Barry's brother. That's the guy we're looking for!" he said, excitedly.

"Watch," said the voice.

Tavus watched as time sped up in the scene. Light seeped into the room from around the edges of the blinds. The boy continued to sleep, perfectly still.

A woman entered the room and approached the window. She drew up the blinds and whispered a good morning in the boy's ear. Her smile was pleasant, her eyes loving.

The boy continued to sleep, perfectly still.

The woman reached over to the nightstand and clicked off the alarm clock. As she did, she wagged her finger at the boy and playfully scolded him.

He didn't move.

This bothered the woman. She touched his shoulders and nudged him.

He didn't awaken.

She shook him.

He didn't awaken.

There was no sound, but Tavus could tell she was screaming for him to wake up as she shook him frantically. Another human, a man, raced into the room. Tavus knew it was the father. He attempted to awaken the boy.

The father tried breathing life into the boy's lungs. Nothing happened. The scene dissolved into darkness as the mother and father held each other and sobbed.

"Spencer had a weak heart. He died in his sleep," said the voice.

"But Barry is convinced his brother is here!" argued the banshee.

"Only an echo, a shadow, of the brother is here. It's a trick to bring light into darkness. Go to your friends and tell them the night is not to be trusted. Go!"

The rock underneath Tavus cracked open and blackness poured forth like lava. He jumped back as a dark creature leaped at him.

"Drats! Looks like you've finally seen the truth! Guess that means lights out for you, Banshee," said the gremlin.

"What?" The banshee flapped his wings and attempted to take to the air.

Swinky smiled. "I love when they put up a fight." The gremlin's clawed fingers wrapped around the banshee's throat as the two of them fell back into the waters of the Dream Stream.

CHAPTER THIRTY-FIVE
PILLOW TALK

STARRY HAD REJECTED EVERY offer made by the Nightmare Squire. The ruler of the Dream Stream had presented him a towering meal of delicious thacky-wack beetles and grickle cucumbers, but the monster had refused. He had offered Starry a soft bed to rest his eyes, but Starry had declined. The latest—and oddest—suggestion was a bedtime story. Starry was bewildered.

"Oh, come now. You mean you wouldn't like to hear a good fairy tale or a fable before catching a few winks?" said the Nightmare Squire.

"No, thank you," said the older monster.

He waved about a book featuring a green monster atop a donkey. "I do wonderful voices. You should hear my ogre. I make my voice very deep and add just a hint of a whiny Scottish accent," said the squire.

"Look, I really don't want you to read me anything," said

Starry. "I just want to wait for my friends to return."

The Nightmare Squire stuck a steaming cup of hot chocolate in front of Starry. "A mug of my personal favorite will really do you good," he said.

Starry looked at him with a menacing eye.

The Nightmare Squire engaged in a series of very dramatic yawns. "Oh, my bones are so achy." He stretched and yawned again. "I imagine your joints could use a rest. A monster your age probably isn't used to all this running around, am I right?" The Nightmare Squire waved his hands, and a large chair with plump cushions dropped out of the Dream Stream and landed before Starry. Gentle music began playing in the cavern.

Starry allowed a yawn to sneak out. He was rather tired.

The Nightmare Squire continued to talk, dropping his volume to a soothing whisper. "The throw pillows are scented. Just take a little nap, and I'll be sure to wake you when your friends return."

"I don't know." Starry yawned three times in a row. His eyelids felt heavy.

"I guarantee you sweet dreams. I mean, how could you go wrong? The ruler of the Dream Stream is promising you the most heavenly slumber you've ever had. Just lay your head on the pillows, Starry."

Starry yawned and stretched, wiggling his tails with pleasure. He hadn't realized how relaxing the squire's voice was. It tinkled like tiny bells after every word.

The Nightmare Squire gently lifted the monster onto the pillows arranged artfully on the chair. He patted the monster on his head and whispered, "A nap, a simple nap, to rest your tired eyes, Starry."

The monster closed his eyes and fell asleep. Soon, his heavy snores echoed throughout the cavern.

The Nightmare Squire smiled. "My pillow talk gets them every time!" He smirked at the sleeping monster and dove into the Dream Stream.

It was time to put an end to his troubles and move forward with his plan. The waters of the Dream Stream slid off his body like oil and water.

CHAPTER THIRTY-SIX
FROM OUT OF THE SHADOWS

THE CREATURES HAD THEM surrounded. The Spencer thing reached for Barry. Max batted its arm away. His hand burned where he had touched the dark creature.

"Oh, do put up a fight! Give my wraiths a reason to slice you to pieces," said Headmaster Stevens.

Paul stuttered, "W-what's going on here?"

The headmaster again smiled and clacked his black teeth together. "You walked into a trap, children."

Barry whispered to the creature who looked like his brother, "Spencer, what did they do to you?"

The creature slapped the boy across the cheeks. "Foolish child, I am not your brother. I am fashioned from his image out of the stuff of nightmares, just to lure you here."

Paul shook his head. "Headmaster, do something! You're scaring the boy!"

The headmaster sighed. "That's the trouble with monsters

these days. Everybody's going all soft. Where did we go wrong? Why are so many perfectly good monsters cursed to be so blasted sensitive?"

"Paul, you're making him angry," muttered Max.

"And to think the Nightmare Squire actually thought you were Dreamkiller material! I told him you were too good, too pure." The headmaster turned his back on his former students. "But does he listen to me?"

"Dreamkillers? What?" said Paul.

"Why, yes, dear Paul. The Nightmare Squire is looking to hire graduates from my Monster Academy. Officially, he'll tell you you're joining his Terror Troops, but you're really becoming something far more sinister."

"I don't understand," said Paul.

Headmaster Stevens huffed, "Do try to follow along, will you? Your teachers always did tell me you had a terrible habit of drifting during lectures."

Paul stood silent.

"Since you won't be leaving the Dream Stream alive, I'll fill you in on our lovely plan. That way, you will die knowing you could do nothing to stop the most unspeakable evil in Cascade's history from entering the world!" The headmaster cleared his throat and shifted his hands to the small of his back as he began his lecture. "I've a confession. I'm not a true monster. I'm a wraith, as are my brothers surrounding you. We are creatures made from the shadows of nightmares. Our master, the Nightmare Squire, took over the Dream Stream for one purpose: to blacken it into a transit of evil. Once he's poisoned all of the Dream Stream with the blackest of nightmares, he will spill forth into the waking world and make it his dark kingdom as well."

"But, why were you put in charge of our school?" asked Max.

"We intend to use the academy as a breeding ground for more Dreamkillers."

"Yeah, you mentioned those Dreamkillers before. I'm a little fuzzy on what you mean by that," said Max.

"Dreamkillers are soldiers of the Nightmare Squire who enter the Dream Stream. They destroy the sickly goodness of dreams and replace them with the horrors of nightmares. It was easy to take over your school and change the textbooks to educate a far more vicious and brutal class of monsters. Some of your classmates have already become very successful as Dreamkillers. In fact, kill enough dreams and you become a glorious wraith." The headmaster lifted his head with immense pride.

"But how does Barry figure in this?" asked Paul. "He's just a boy."

"That I'm not sure about. Our master is somehow threatened by the human. I don't know why. He looks useless and weak." The headmaster scratched his knuckles with his long claws, which appeared twice as long as Paul and Max remembered. "Wouldn't make much of a meal for anyon—"

A horrible wail interrupted the headmaster. Crashing onto the plateau from above came a very battered banshee. He landed on a pair of wraiths near Max.

The wraiths tossed the banshee into the circle.

Paul cried out, "Tavus, you came back!"

Tavus looked up at his monster friends. His left eye was badly bruised. "I have to tell you guys something! You're in incredible trouble!"

The headmaster smiled and approached the banshee. "And what truth do you know, little bird-boy?"

Tavus pointed to the Spencer look-alike. "That's not Barry's brother. It's a fake."

The Spencer wraith laughed heartily.

The headmaster's cackle joined in. He hunched over the banshee and whispered, "I'm afraid you're a little late with the news. Guess the truth won't set you free. You'll always be the boy who can't be trusted. See what crying wolf does to you?"

"Step away from him!" demanded Paul. He stood with his feet firmly planted.

Max rushed over to the banshee. "Are you okay?"

"I'm fine. Had a fight with a nasty gremlin. Barely won. Don't know how I got here." The banshee sounded exhausted.

"Sorry I was late with the news. I'm such a waste."

Max lifted him up and placed him on his shoulders. "Nonsense. We're glad you're here." He looked around at the wraiths. "We can use all the help we can get."

"Enough chatter. Let's finish this!" shouted Headmaster Stevens. He barked at his fellow wraiths, "I don't care who eats the boy or the banshee. Just steer clear of the monsters. Max and Paul are mine!" The headmaster's mouth opened wide as he rushed toward Paul.

CHAPTER THIRTY-SEVEN
I SCREAM, YOU SCREAM

THE WRAITHS POURED OVER their victims. The Spencer thing charged at Barry, who stood frozen. Max swept his left foot around and landed a powerful kick to the ribs of the aggressive wraith. His foot flew through the shadow thing like it was made of paper and the wraith split in half. Not phased by its current state, the creature slid its legs back to its waist and reattached itself. Barry looked away from the horrible sight.

"Oh, great. They can grow back together!" Max shouted.

Paul was holding the headmaster's wrists, fighting to keep the menacing claws from reaching his slender and very exposed neck.

The banshee atop Max screamed at the wraiths. His ear-piercing scream numbed Max, especially with the banshee so close to his ears.

Max pawed at the banshee. "Hey, my eardrums are next door here. A little consideration!"

The wraiths near the banshee retreated, their shapes wiggling at the edges.

Max saw what was happening. "Ignore that last order. Scream your heart out, Tavus! Looks like these creeps don't care for your singing voice!"

Tavus took to the air and flew toward the wraiths. They shrunk back even further, the shadow stuff of their bodies melting into each other. They abandoned the plateau and scampered down the side to safety.

Tavus circled around. All but two wraiths had been chased away. The fake Spencer and the headmaster stood back to back, eyeing the banshee with distaste.

"We have to get out of here!" said Paul. He moved toward Barry who had crumpled to the ground and lay curled up. He was sobbing and quivering. "I think Barry went into shock!"

"Which way is out?" asked Max.

The headmaster seemed to be discussing a plan of attack with the other wraith. Paul didn't like the determination and hatred that dwelled in their faces.

"I don't see an exit anywhere. Where's the hose thingie we jumped through to get here?" asked Paul as he scanned the skies for any sign of an opening.

A familiar voice echoed through the minds of Paul and Max. "Just follow the light."

"What?" said Max.

"Oh, my gosh! It's Bickyl! He's here!" said Paul.

Appearing suddenly in the sky was their dragon friend. He glided over their heads, his entire body glowing a bright yellow.

"Why's he glowing? He can do that?" asked Max.

"Uh, I didn't think so." Paul watched the brilliant dragon soar through the air.

The dragon wheeled around and returned, angling his tail toward them. "Go to the light, my tail light!" The dragon's thoughts were filled with their usual warmth, plus something else, but Paul couldn't tell what.

Paul looked at Barry. Max shouted over the banshee's screaming. "I'll get Barry. Jump on!"

Paul leaped up and snatched hold of the dragon's scaly tail. Max hoisted up Barry and grabbed the dragon's tail one-handed.

The dragon sent his thoughts to the banshee. "Little flyer, you must be touching me when I leave this place or you'll be left behind."

"I will," the banshee replied, ceasing his screaming for but a few seconds.

That was the opening the wraiths below needed. As the dragon's tail dragged off the plateau, the Spencer thing leaped up, grabbing hold of Barry's backpack.

The wraith's lips curled up, forming a toothless smile. "Brother, it's me. I'm not a wraith. They changed me into that thing. I'm me! I'm your brother!"

A faint smile lit up Barry's face. "Spence!"

The dragon's thoughts blazed a warning. "Hold tight! I'm taking us back to the Dream Stream and away from this dark place!"

Bickyl dragged his friends to safety, unaware of the evil hitchhiker in tow.

CHAPTER THIRTY-EIGHT
STREAM OF UNCONSCIOUSNESS

THE DRAGON SWAM THROUGH the Dream Stream against the current. He was heading downward with determination. Dreams and nightmares flew by in a blur as Bickyl sliced through the waters.

"Bickyl's taking us upstream!" said Paul.

"Mighty odd stuff, going down to head upstream." Max chuckled at his quirky observation.

"Get away from him!" said Tavus, glaring at the wraith attached to Barry. Tavus tried to scream to knock the creature loose, but the banshee found while he could talk in the Dream Stream, his scream didn't work. Tavus tried kicking the Spencer imitation.

Barry squealed, "Stop it! He's my brother, you stupid monster!"

"I need my concentration. Going against the flow is not easy." Bickyl's thoughts washed over all of their minds.

"Where are we going?" asked Paul. He too wanted to dispose of their hitchhiker, but knew the dragon needed to be free of distractions. Once they arrived at their destination, they could take fight off the wraith. Paul looked down at the creepy version of Spencer. It wouldn't hurt Barry as long as he was the only thing linking the evil shadow to the dragon.

"To the heart of the matter. We are going to the headwaters of the Dream Stream. The truth, as well as your parts in this adventure, will be revealed." The dragon's thoughts were coated with sincerity.

"You sound different," said Paul.

"I am changed. When you entered the Dream Stream, I was returning to the Dream Mesa after leading away those twirly thorns. In my mind, I felt danger brewing for you. I blasted upward, flying above the Dream Mesa. Pouring forth from the mesa's top was the Dream Stream. I entered the waterway, hoping to find and rescue you."

"Took you long enough," said Max.

"Instead, the Dream Stream directed me to her headwaters. I sensed urgency and a connection to your troubles." The dragon veered to the left, avoiding a large black patch of fouled water. "At the headwaters, the Dream Stream revealed her secrets. She showed me what we need to do."

"Wait, I'm confused. Is the Dream Stream the same as the Nightmare Squire? If it is, we don't want anything to do with that bozo." Max hugged the dragon's tail and ducked, avoiding a baby carriage loaded with yo-yos speeding by.

"No, they are not the same. Trust me. We will be there soon and you will know what comes next." The dragon accelerated his descent.

****

Behind them, a dark batch of water spilled forth its contents. The Nightmare Squire oozed out, carrying Headmaster Stevens and an unconscious Swinky in his arms. "We need to put an end to this nonsense," he hissed. "You two better hope your mistakes don't ruin my plan."

Headmaster Stevens shivered. Despite his own evilness, his master easily stirred up fears in his black heart.

From out of the black patch, over a dozen wraiths joined their master, clouding the Dream Stream with their evil.

CHAPTER THIRTY-NINE
HALF SPENCE NONE THE RICHER

THE HEADWATERS WERE CLEANER than any other part of the stream they had seen. Paul looked around and saw no evidence of the black patches that speckled the rest of the Dream Stream. There was a pureness to the place. It was holy and sacred. Feelings of warmth washed over him as the dragon exited the waters and deposited them onto a beach of white sand. Paul looked all around and saw endless dunes of sand stretching to the horizon. Only the rising tower of the Dream Stream stood out at the center of the beach.

Paul and Max slid off the dragon's tail. Treek slid out from his hiding place in Paul's vest and wrapped himself around his owner's neck. The tiny pet was very rattled by its trip into the Dream Stream.

Tavus flew for the Spencer thing as soon as Barry was safely dropped onto the sand. The wraith hid behind the boy.

"Barry, he's gonna kill me!" screeched the creature.

Barry tossed sand at the banshee. "Stay away from me and my brother!"

"It's not your brother, Barry! That thing is impersonating him!" The banshee landed a few yards from Barry.

Barry said, "That's wrong. He's Spencer. We were supposed to go to the Dream Mesa and find him. We did, and now we can go home." He looked up at his older brother.

The Spencer creep smiled, being careful not to reveal his black teeth behind his lips. "We can do whatever you want, Barry. Don't listen to that banshee."

The boy turned away from Tavus and spoke to his brother with excitement. "We can go home now. Mom and Dad will be so glad to see you," Barry said.

Spencer nodded.

Tavus had to tell the boy. He sensed that this was the right place. Honesty would ring true here, at the headwaters of the Dream Stream. He had to make Barry believe him. "Barry, your brother is here. He will always be here in the Dream Stream for you, but he can't be with you. That thing is not your brother. It's a twisted echo of him."

Barry looked at Tavus. The child's large eyes were downcast.

Tavus continued, "The Dream Stream told me this. Spencer didn't run away. He didn't leave you on purpose." The banshee stepped closer. "Your brother had a weak heart. He died in his sleep. Barry, deep in your heart, you know this is the truth."

"No! That's not what happened. He ran off to this magical place. He went here so we could have an adventure. It was a game, right, Spence?" Barry looked into the shadow thing's eyes.

"That isn't your brother," said Tavus.

"Mom and Dad would tell me if you died. They wouldn't lie." Tears began to stream from Barry's eyes.

"That's not your brother. It's a shadow of your brother. The Nightmare Squire created him from nightmares. It might contain a tiny bit of your brother, but it's not him."

"They wouldn't lie." Barry sank to his knees.

Barry was believing the banshee, but at what cost. Tavus did not like to see his words unravel someone in such a way. He placed a hand on the child's left shoulder.

From behind them, clapping echoed. They turned to see the Nightmare Squire step out of the Dream Stream. He did not set foot on the sand, but hovered a few feet from its purity. "What a touching scene!"

A black cloud of wraiths filled the sky. More had joined their master as he had traveled through the Dream Stream. In front, Headmaster Stevens and a now awake Swinky stood sneering.

The wraith pretending to be Spencer slashed his claws downward and across the forearm of the banshee. Tavus screamed in pain, his blood staining the white sand.

Spencer grabbed Barry and yanked him into the air. He joined his master at his side, clamping down hard on Barry's pinwheeling arms.

Paul screamed, "No!"

"It appears the upper hand is once again mine!" The Nightmare Squire waved to his horde of wraiths, which had grown in number to well over several dozen. "Dreamkillers, do your jobs! And please, be messy about it!"

CHAPTER FORTY
IT'S ALWAYS DARKEST...

THE ATTACKING WRAITHS WERE halted by a blast of white flames from Bickyl. The dragon stood in front of his friends and glared up at the Nightmare Squire.

"Call them off!" His words blasted through everyone's heads.

Max whispered to Paul, "I thought he wasn't a fire-breather. What's up with that?"

"I don't know. It must be the Dream Stream!" Paul supported the wounded banshee who leaned against him.

"Dragon, step away. A few silly flames will not discourage my soldiers." The Nightmare Squire barked orders at the wraiths.

They dove toward Paul and Max.

Bickyl poured white flames at them. Upon impacting with the shadows, the creatures burst into dust.

This horrified the Nightmare Squire. "That's not possible.

You can't do that. The only thing that can destroy a nightmare..."

A voice echoed through the sky. "Is the purity of a dream."

Paul and Max exchanged questioning looks.

Recognizing the voice, Tavus said, "That's the Dream Stream."

The voice continued, "You have polluted my waters for too long, beast! You should never have come to my headwaters! Bickyl is filled with dreams. He is one of my protectors now!"

"Yes, the headwaters are your place of strength. Blah-blah! Foolish one, I would only come here if I had gathered enough darkness to destroy you. More nightmares run through the Dream Stream now than your pathetic dreams. My Dreamkillers have done their job well. With every dream they ended, a nightmare rose to take its place. I come here now, strong enough to make all of the Dream Stream mine!" He pointed a fist at the sand beneath him. A thick tentacle of darkness uncurled and struck the white dunes. Where it touched, blackness began to spread.

The Dream Stream's voice faltered. "Light and dark must exist together. Hopes and fears must dance through the minds of the sleeping."

"Bah, I've had enough with the idea of balance. Power is worth having only when one has more of it. Today, I am filled with power. Today, you sided with children." The Nightmare Squire yanked Barry from the clutches of the Spencer wraith. "Weak things that curl up into little balls when night falls."

"Spencer, help me," Barry pleaded to the wraith.

The shadow thing that impersonated Spencer hissed at Barry, gnashing his black teeth at him.

The boy began to cry.

"See how he cowers?" said the Nightmare Squire. "You ally yourself with nothing. And you sent me dreams that made me fear this sniveling child?" The Nightmare Squire laughed. "You actually had me spooked. He is nothing. He is just a whiny, ordinary boy. It was so easy to lure them here." The Nightmare Squire's body swirled about, forming a cloud of mist that gradually took on the image of the Wizard Bailey. "It was child's play to imitate a foolish wizard. You trusting fools fell right into my trap."

Paul's jaw dropped. It was the wizard who had appeared so conveniently at Periphery Point. Starry had sensed something wrong about the wizard, and he had been right.

The Nightmare Squire tossed Barry to the sand below. He landed in a patch of white surrounded by the growing darkness. Barry looked up at the icy eyes of the Nightmare Squire.

The ground underneath the boy rose upward, thrusting to the sky and creating a small mesa ten feet in height. It brought the child to the same level as the Nightmare Squire. Barry sat at its center, his eyes wide.

The Dream Stream said, "Barry, you are an ordinary boy and that makes you special. By nature, boys and girls are filled with dreams. The magic of dreams is never more powerful than when you are young. You were brought here by the Nightmare Squire because he feared you and he felt that squelching your most heartfelt dream would empower him. Show him there is nothing to fear from dreams."

"I don't understand. He's too mean," said Barry. He looked down at Paul and his other monster friends. Their eyes were filled with hope.

Barry shook his head, his mind frozen.

"The Nightmare Squire wasn't created to be scary and cruel. One grows into the role of evil. He was once a child filled with a balance of dreams and nightmares." Bickyl's warm voice eased into the boy's mind. "Show him your hopes. Reach out and show him dreams cannot die, little one. Show him Spencer lives on."

Barry allowed a tear to escape before closing his eyes and stretching his hands out to the Nightmare Squire. White rays of dream material skipped through the air and enveloped the Nightmare Squire.

Barry felt his hopes and dreams pouring forth from him and into the Nightmare Squire. He was sharing his dreams.

All around the Nightmare Squire, the dream images danced. The ruler of the Dream Stream twisted his head back at an impossible angle and clawed at his skull. His dark eyes displayed fear.

Inside the squire's mind, Barry's dreams were eating through the blackness. One dream in particular cast the brightest light on the darkness. Barry joined his older brother in a land of pastel clouds and rainbow-colored birds. The boys smiled and played together with the pure energy of children.

Dreams of rocket trips to the moon and the tender hugs of a mother, of flying cars and lazy summer fishing trips with a loving dad shattered the Nightmare Squire's dark armor. His power was not drained from him. Deep inside the Nightmare Squire, light and dark twisted into the shape of a delicate flower, each petal changing constantly from black to white. The pattern spread outward, transforming the Nightmare Squire into a being full of both dreams and nightmares. He shrank in height until he was no taller than Barry. His black tangle of hair swirled about forming into a mop of brown bangs. Freckles dotted his chubby cheeks as a button nose found a home in the middle of his face. His black teeth disappeared, replaced by white teeth capped with shiny braces. A black T-shirt wrapped itself around him as denim jeans cascaded down his legs. Impossibly clean white sneakers slid over his feet.

Barry opened his eyes and looked at the Nightmare Squire with astonishment. Standing in front of him was a boy, whose eyes were filled with the nervous energy of fears and dreams.

Barry reached out an open hand "I'm Barry. What's your name?"

The Nightmare Squire smiled, catching his top lip slightly on his braces. He touched his teeth and searched his mind for his name. "I think I'm the Dream Prince. I don't have a name, only a title."

Barry bit his lip. "How about we call you Spence?"

"I'd like that," said Spence.

All around the boys, the darkness of the wraiths and whiteness of the sands had mixed to form a beach that resembled fudge ripple ice cream. The headwaters of the Dream Stream had been restored.

Farther up in the Dream Stream, the black patches were gone. Its waters glistened a deep, dark blue, the perfect balance of light and dark.

The waterway of imagination once again flowed pure.

CHAPTER FORTY-ONE
ON A STARRY NIGHT...

BICKYL FLEW EVERYONE ON his back, a feat that always impressed Paul. Barry and the Dream Prince sat up near the dragon's head, followed by Paul and Max. A much mellower Swinky sat behind them, arguing with Tavus about who was the bigger spinner of tall tales. The gremlin still served the cause of nightmares, but was far less cruel, following the lead of his new master.

They flew upward, leaving the headwaters of the Dream Stream behind. All around them, the waters seemed filled with renewed energy and purpose. Dream images, as well as nightmare visions, swam by past in large numbers.

They emerged from the Dream Stream inside the grand central cavern of the Dream Mesa. Bickyl landed next to a large cushioned chair, waking the groggy monster who protested with an annoyed yawn.

Starry grumbled, "It's about time you found your way back."

Barry raced over to his monster and delivered a crushing hug. "We did it!"

Starry huffed, "Ease up. You're making me see stars!" The older monster coughed as Barry dropped him to the safety of the throw pillows. "So, you found Spencer?"

Barry nodded solemnly. "I know where he is now."

Starry smiled weakly and directed his question to Paul. "He learned what happened to Spence?"

"He knows Spencer died," said Paul. He hesitated, then inquired, "You knew all along, didn't you?"

Starry said, "That's why I chose to befriend him rather than haunt him."

"You look old. Can I swing you around by your tails?" asked Spence.

"Who's this?" asked Starry, tucking his tails underneath.

Barry said, "Um, that's the new Spence. It's really that scary Nightmare guy. I think I changed him back to a kid."

Starry looked lost. "What happened in there?"

Bickyl explained, "The Nightmare Squire had grown full of evil. He sought to overrun the waters of the Dream Stream with nightmares, thereby killing all the dreams. Barry showed him the power contained in hope and brought the squire back into balance. He reverted back to a young age where his good and evil natures are more equal." The dragon observed the boy attempting to snatch one of Starry's tails. "I suspect he'll be filled with all sorts of mischief."

"But, why did Barry call him Spence? Spencer doesn't look like that," said Starry.

"Let me help, master," offered Swinky. The gremlin jumped to assist Spence.

Starry tried to bury his backside in the pillows.

"I think Barry wanted to honor his brother," said Paul. Free from the Dream Stream, Treek was racing up and down his owner's small frame, licking him with joy.

"Are all those wraiths gone?" asked Max.

Before responding, the dragon blew a warm blast of air at Tavus who was shivering cold from their swim in the waters. "I think so. They were created in hate, and when the hate left the Nightmare Squire, the wraiths disappeared."

"Even Headmaster Stevens?" asked Paul.

"Yes, I think so," said the dragon. "Understand that the Dream Stream told me much, but not everything."

Starry, hearing about the headmaster, said, "I knew that headmaster wasn't right. There's your reason why the handbook was messed up."

Paul and Max nodded.

"I can't believe they actually removed chapters and were solely teaching evilness and scare tactics. If I was in charge of that school…"

Paul's eyes lit up. "Hey, why don't you?"

Starry said, "What?"

"Well, the headmaster position is open, and you'd be perfect for the job." Paul hopped up and down, excited at his idea.

Max added, "You would be good for the job. Headmasters should be a perfect mix of thoughtfulness and grumpiness. You already have the grumpy part mastered."

Starry ignored Max. "Maybe I could do it. Definitely getting too old to be reassigned to another child."

Barry said, "What do you mean, Starry? Are you done with me?"

Starry hopped off the chair, gracefully slapping Spence and Swinky with his tails before landing in Barry's lap. "I think our time is over. You've dealt with a lot, and it's time to bond with your foster parents instead of me. You need the comfort of a family, not a closet monster."

Barry's eyes began to water. "I don't want you to go."

"I have to, Barry. It's time." Starry's lips quivered as the monster struggled to contain his own sadness.

Barry hugged the monster. "I'll never forget you."

Starry said, "I know. I'm pretty unforgettable." He smiled

and patted Barry with his tails.

All was quiet in the Dream Mesa as the boy and his monster held each other.

The Dream Prince broke the silence. "If he doesn't need you, I do, Barry."

Barry stared at the Dream Prince. "What do you mean?"

"I remember what I became. I don't want to grow up and be another Nightmare Squire. I think you can help me. Will you stay here in the Dream Mesa and rule the Dream Stream by my side?" The Dream Prince's eyes sparkled with hope and uncertainty.

Barry stood speechless at the invitation.

CHAPTER FORTY-TWO
DREAM JOBS

IT WAS AN EXTRAORDINARY offer. The chance to help rule the world of dreams and nightmares didn't come up in casual conversation very often. Co-piloting the stories dancing about in the minds of the sleeping was a golden opportunity for anyone with imagination. Barry had creativity galore.

The Dream Prince added, "When you shared your dreams with me, they were so bright and full of life. I know you can help me keep the Dream Stream on the right track. What do you say?"

"What about his parents? He can't just disappear. They'd worry themselves to death," argued Starry.

"Maybe he could help Spencer without leaving his home." Bickyl's voice tickled Barry's head.

"What do you mean?" asked Paul and Max at the same time.

Bickyl stretched his wings as he broadcast his thoughts. "Barry could assist the Dream Prince through his dreams."

Spence said, "I don't quite know what I'm doing. I have some of the Nightmare Squire's memories, but how to run the Dream Stream isn't one of them."

"No surprise there. The creep didn't know how to properly manage the place himself," said Starry.

"You may not yet know how to maintain the balance of the Dream Stream, but you could enter the stream and visit Barry in his dreams. There, you could compare ideas and talk about the right decisions that would retain harmony between fear and fancy." The dragon curled his tail around Barry and Spencer, drawing them closer to each other. "It would be a dream job."

"I'll do it," said Barry, hugging the Dream Prince.

The dragon lowered his head. "And with your permission, Prince, I would be honored if you'd let me assist in protecting you and the Dream Stream."

Paul said, "Hey, Bickyl, that'd be a perfect job for you! You would be guarding something much more precious than a pile of riches."

Bickyl winked at his monster friend. "I know. It would make my parents proud and also make me feel like I was making a difference."

Max said, "Well, that's all fine and dandy. Barry has a great job he can do in his sleep. Starry's all set up over at the Monster Academy. What about Paul and me? There's no way we're going back to our jobs. That sock drawer was no fun at all."

Bickyl sighed. "I have the perfect position for the two of you." The dragon looked to the Dream Prince. "With your approval, I think these two would make excellent Nightmare Advisors. They could help you fashion scary visions, yet keep them from being too cruel and evil. What do you think?"

"Sounds great. The more friends I have helping me, the better." He looked at the sneaky gremlin at his side. "That includes you, Swinky. Your heart is filled with mischief, which will keep things interesting."

"It would be an honor, young Prince," said the gremlin, bowing.

Tavus spoke next. "You sure you can trust that goon? He was pretty nasty to me earlier."

The Dream Prince approached the banshee, who kept a safe range from Swinky. "His heart is no longer clouded with darkness. He deserves a second chance."

The banshee nodded.

Paul said, "If we're gonna be employed by you, we need titles, sir."

"How about Assistant Directors of Dire Dreams?" Max puffed out his chest with pride.

"Works for me," said Paul. "I kind of like working so close to water." He held up a webbed hand.

While Paul and Max started grumbling to the Dream Prince about adequate office space, Bickyl took Starry on his back for a ride over the Dream Mesa to fill him in on the mess awaiting him at the academy.

Tavus, however, sulked behind a large rock. Barry walked over to try and cheer up the banshee. "What's wrong?"

The banshee stammered, "Everyone has a place here, but me. I'm returning to a village that thinks I'm a liar. I'm sure when I tell them what happened on our adventure, my bad reputation will be stronger than ever. There's no way they'll believe me."

"Well, then that's our first job before all others," said Barry. "I'm sure everyone would be happy to return to your village and backup your story."

"Really? You'd do that for me?" said Tavus.

"Of course! That's what friends are for." Barry smiled.

The banshee returned a wide smile.

"C'mon, we'd better get over there." Barry jerked his thumb at Paul and Max, who had the Dream Prince cornered against the cavern wall. "Those two can wear anyone down."

"Wow! We get to save the Dream Prince twice in one day,"

remarked Tavus, taking to the air.

Barry laughed and raced after the banshee. He deeply missed his brother, but knew now that he had the strength to go on. He knew he would meet Spencer again. After all, anything is possible in the world of dreams. He refocused his attention on his new friend.

The Dream Prince was younger, and Barry could tell he needed someone to be an older brother. That's an important job. Barry hoped he was ready for the task. He wanted to make Spencer proud.

He let a tear escape from the corner of his eye. It fell downward until it hit the Dream Stream. Merging with the waters of the stream, it flowed upward, its destination—the stars.

Special Thanks Department

My wife, Michelle, pushed so many priorities aside to edit the script in detail. Her keen eye for clarity and editing talents have made it the strong story it is now.
Thank you, Michelle.

Mary Guiffré is a former student with a wonderful imagination. She devours books and assists me after school once a week with school activities. She helped me immensely by offering her young reader perspective on this book. Each week, I handed her new pages of the story with excitement. Knowing she was coming each week to eagerly read what I had written made me stick to a solid schedule and finish this complex novel. I deeply appreciate her thoughtful comments, questions and advice.
Thank you, Mary.

Printed in the United States
22235LVS00001B/298